SHAKESPEARE'S SECRETS:
ROMEO & JULIET

SHAKESPEARE'S SECRETS: ROMEO & JULIET

ESSAYS AND REFLECTIONS ON SHAKESPEARE'S ROMEO AND JULIET

David Blixt

(Formerly titled "Origin of the Feud")
Copyright (C) 2012 David Blixt
Layout design and Copyright (C) 2019 Creativia
Published 2019 by Creativia
Edited by Wicked Words Editing
Cover art by Cover Mint
All rights reserved. No part of this book may be reproduced or transmitted in any form or by any means, electronic or mechanical, including photocopying, recording, or by any information storage and retrieval system, without the author's permission.
The essays in this collection are based on my theatrical experience. I've been incredibly lucky to work with some of the best directors and performers of Shakespeare in the world. To them I can say only thanks, and thanks.
http://www.davidblixt.com/

Contents

Foreword	1
I Always Hated Shakespeare	3
Origin of the Feud	12
Sources	16
Don't Believe the Title	25
The Prologue	29
The Real Capulets & Montagues of Verona	32
Draw Thy Tool	36
The Juliet Trap	40
Mab	44
It's Not a Masked Ball!	50
Redeeming Romeo	54

The Window Scene	62
The King and the Beggar	71
Ratcatcher	79
The Art of Mis-timing Part I	83
The Quartet	87
Family Dysfunction	97
Tybalt's Ghost	101
She's Not Dead Yet!	102
The Art of Mis-timing Part II	110
The Friar's Guilt	114
The Death of Benvolio	118
Loving Lady Montague	120
Favorite Play	123
A Prayer Before Dying	127
Coffee with the Count	131
Resources	140
Author Biography	143
Other Books by David Blixt	145

Foreword

Shakespeare's play about the star-cross'd lovers has dominated my life for over twenty-five years. I have been involved with more than thirty productions, directing my fair share of them. I often joke that I know the play better than I know most people.

Love of the play led me to a love of Verona, a vibrant city where all the classical monuments are still in use today. In 2014, Verona's mayor flew my wife and me out for the release of the Italian edition of my first novel and to speak about that wonderful nexus of history and theatre where I reside. We're friends with Veronese filmmakers, professors, singers, footballers, sword fighters, and even nobility.

All of this stems from *Romeo and Juliet*.

When I first released my thoughts on R&J as an e-book in 2012, it was a lark, a way to combine some old essays I'd written into something like a coherent whole and thus promote my novels. I couldn't conceive it would take on a life of its own.

Five years on, asked to release a print edition, I felt the need to bulk it up. This forced me to go back to the play once more and look at all the things I take for granted, as well as do additional research to hunt sources for several of my assertions. This led to a lot of new material, including several fresh discoveries on my part. That's what I love about Shakespeare: There's always something new to explore, even in a play I know so intimately.

There are ten additional chapters in this edition, and there's not a single chapter from the original version that did not undergo revisions. There was a metric ton of new research, but there have also been many more years of producing and performing this show, with new casts and new directors, all of whom offer fresh perspectives.

This is not meant to be an authoritative how-to for approaching *Romeo and Juliet* so much as a collection of thoughts from someone who has spent his entire adult life marinating in this play, year after year. In fact, since I was seventeen, there has not been a single year when Verona, Mantua, Padua, or Venice has not been part of my existence. Romeo, Juliet, and Verona have dominated my thoughts for so long that I cannot imagine my life without them.

So allow me to share a few of those thoughts with you. Some are original, while most are stolen from better minds than mine. All of them deal with Verona's most famous citizens, who never existed save in legend.

Enjoy!

I Always Hated Shakespeare

Shakespeare's *Romeo and Juliet* and How the
Capulet-Montague Feud Inspired a Series of Novels

I always hated Shakespeare.

They made me read him. In junior high, it was *Julius Caesar*, and I hated it. In high school, it was *Romeo and Juliet*, which was cool only because we wasted a week watching the movie (the Zeffirelli, not the DiCaprio). The next year it was Henry IV, Part 1, to which I said, 'You've gotta be kidding,' and scraped through by listening to class discussions.

The Bard of Avon and I were not friendly. So how did I happen to write *The Master of Verona*, the first of my *Star-Cross'd* series, combining so many of his characters and plays into one grand tapestry?

It started my senior year of high school. I had a choice between a reading-Shakespeare and an acting-Shakespeare class. I'd done some acting, and there were no quizzes involved in the performance class. A no-brainer.

It got better when I was cast as Mercutio. Perhaps the best role for a young man, he has all the best dirty lines, a great ambiguous speech, a good fight, and a great death, then backstage to play cards until curtain call. What more could one want?

Somewhere in the middle of rehearsals, I realized that my teachers had been holding out on me for years. Shakespeare wasn't an author. He was a playwright. He didn't write literature. He wrote plays, words to be spoken on stage by real, living actors.

It was like the sun had come out. You don't read Shakespeare. You perform him.

Thus started my love affair with Shakespeare. Community theatre, college productions, professional summer-stock, and rep companies until finally I was performing with some of the greatest Shakespearean actors in the world. I became a Shakespearean actor, something I would never have believed.

Shakespeare gave me a career. Then he did me one better and introduced me to my wife. We met playing Kate and Petruchio in *The Taming of the Shrew*, giving us banter material for the rest of our lives. Today, she's the Artistic Director of the Michigan Shakespeare Festival and the Executive Director of A Crew Of Patches Theatre Company, while I bum around acting and choreographing stage violence. Performing and directing Shakespeare pays our bills.

Then, as if icing this cake with the word irony, Shakespeare got me to write a book. Once again, it starts with *Romeo and Juliet*.

I've shared my general thoughts on that play elsewhere, but to boil it down, I'm firmly of the opinion that Shakespeare's play isn't a Tragedy; it's actually a Comedy that goes horribly wrong. These are comic characters (lovesick young man, headstrong young girl, clowns, etc.) doing comic things (falling in and out of love, having secret weddings, etc.), only people begin dying.

I expressed these views at the bar a few times, and before I knew it, I found myself approached to direct the show. Basically a "put your money where your mouth is" proposition.

Warily, I accepted. I was 25, and it was my first time directing Shakespeare. So I pored over the whole text in a way I'd never done as an actor. And while I was doing that, I found something.

I found a cause for the feud.

The show came and went, as all shows do. Throughout the following year, however, I was unable to leave the origin of the feud behind. The play was done, yet my research continued of its own volition.

I'd waded shin-deep into the history of Verona; now, as I completely submerged myself, I discovered some interesting facts.

At the time the tale of the star-cross'd lovers supposedly took place, some important people were in Verona:

Dante, the father of Renaissance literature.

Giotto, the father of Renaissance painting.

Petrarch, the poet who technically started the Renaissance by finding Cicero's letters there.

Looking at those names, I realized that in a very real sense the Renaissance began in Verona at the start of the fourteenth century.

I then read the earlier versions of the play, the short stories (some not so short) that were Shakespeare's sources, and then back further to his sources' sources. I pinpointed a four-year period wherein the tale was supposed to take place — during the reign of one Bartolomeo della Scala, some time between 1300 and 1304. It was the first time I had heard the name della Scala, and I had no idea how much that name would come to dominate my life. Not insignificantly, Shakespeare's Prince in the play is named Escalus, a Latin version of della Scala. I found that Dante had dedicated the third canticle of his Divine Comedy, "Paradiso," to Bartolomeo's younger brother, Cangrande della Scala.

Cangrande. It didn't mean much to me at the time. But it would.

At the same time I was running around doing historical research, I was also reading fiction. I am a glutton for well-written historical fiction. Bernard Cornwell, Patrick O'Brian, Colleen McCullough's *Masters of Rome* series, all of it. At the time, though, at the suggestion of my future wife, I was reading Dorothy Dunnett, perhaps the pinnacle of the genre. Dunnett is the only author who consistently makes me feel stupid—not always a good quality in a writer. You have to earn Dunnett, want Dunnett, especially for the first hundred or so pages. But once you're in her world, there's no going back. She weaves a tapestry so fine, so richly detailed, so at the core of human experience, that her books are each a treasure.

It was Dorothy Dunnett, more than any other writer, who showed me that a book can be smart, dark, witty, gruesome, and exciting all at once. Her death was a heartbreaking loss to literature.

But back in early 2000, I hadn't yet completed even the first of her series of historical novels. I wasn't fully able to enjoy *The Lymond Chronicles* because Dante and the rest of the Verona cast kept getting in my way. So I laid her books aside and started to write.

It was going to be a short book, simple and sweet; it would get the idea out of my system.

Frustration followed. In the first couple of attempts, I couldn't find the voice. I was obsessed with the notion of the feud, which at that time was the core of my book. But it simply wasn't enough. While the origin of the Capulet-Montague feud fascinated me, it was the backdrop — the della Scalas, Giotto, Dante — that kept leaping to the fore.

More research, more false starts. I settled in to read Dante's *Divine Comedy*, something I would have bet money against at any other point in my life. It wasn't the great revelation Shakespeare was, but it did give me the landscape of the time. And halfway through, Dante knocked my socks off by mentioning the feud between the Capelletti and Montecchi families. Capulets and Montagues, anyone?

Yet in reading both the histories and Dante's work, one man's name kept cropping up. A man who stood above all his peers, outshone the luminaries of his day. Giotto's patron, Dante's friend. A man fit to be the tragic hero of one of Shakespeare's plays. His name was Cangrande della Scala, but he was also known as The Greyhound of Verona. Revered as almost a God in his own lifetime, the man took Verona to its highest height, just before its worst fall. Dead before he turned forty, he was successful in everything he did and was a tremendous patron of the arts.

In Cangrande's time, Verona was hated and feared by its neighbors. Venice conspired against Cangrande, as did popes and emperors. There was an almost unceasing war with nearby Padua for the twenty years of his rule, a city he finally won through benevolence, not war. There was the play by Paduan poet Albertino Mussato about Cangrande, veiled as being about someone else, showing him to be a bloody tyrant. Cangrande's life fascinated me as much as any play I'd ever read.

Because he reminded me of someone, a rogue I had fallen in love with the first time I played him. The ties between Shakespeare and Dante were growing.

Soon I was reading about Dante himself — his wit, his loves, his politics, his exile, his family. It was then that it happened — one of those moments you hear writers talk about, when a character steps off the page and introduces himself as the lead. For me, it was Pietro Alighieri, also known as Pietro di Dante. Barely eighteen when my story starts, he came upon the scene and knocked down all my plans, which is very unlike him because he's a good guy. A really good guy. The kind of guy I'd want to play if I didn't enjoy scoundrels so much. Raised in his father's ever-growing shadow, he was a prospectless second son until the death of his elder brother elevated him to heir. With no particular skill in anything, just great heart and determination, he gave my novel its voice. For the sake of my narrative I moved away from Pietro now and again, but Pietro's experience is ours, and we can watch in his growth, feel pride in his achievements, and share his disillusionments.

But there was another element missing. If the idea for the feud was going to become the subplot, a crucial but subdued backdrop, where was my plot? What was my spine? The book seemed to be writing itself, and everything was falling into place, but still I didn't know what Pietro's goal was.

That was when Shakespeare returned. The Bard of Avon seemed to chuckle as he met Dante's son and gave him his *raison d'etre*. For me, it was the ultimate 'duh!' moment. I said earlier that all good directors go back to the text. It appears to go for writers, as well. However it happened, I had come full circle, the best of all possible worlds.

Mercutio. Of course, Mercutio. Referred to both as a cousin to the Prince, and "the Prince's near ally," Mercutio was in some way tied to the della Scala family. The pivotal figure of *Romeo and Juliet* would be only a newborn babe when my story began. We couldn't follow him, not from the outset — following the adventures of a toddler in fourteenth-century Italy is not what I call exciting. But following the trials and tribulations of his protector, young Pietro Alighieri — that had promise.

All at once it was Mercutio's story. The possibility of creating from Shakespeare's text and real history the tale of this marvelously troubled young man was just too tempting. I could explain the darkness in the Queen Mab speech, from his disdain of love and his homoerotic tendencies to his fear of war drums and his foul images of childbirth. As I knew so well as an actor, Shakespeare's Mercutio has a wealth of possibility. If I could tap even a little of it, I had the makings of a great story.

Moreover, bringing it back to Shakespeare led me to look at the phrase 'star-cross'd,' which carries both prophecy and futility, as if nothing can be done to alter the lovers' dark fate. But in fact, Mercutio is the agent of the stars because his death is what leads the young lovers to their fate. So Mercutio is a tool of the heavens.

Dante uses prophecy often. *Inferno* begins with a retooling of an ancient prophecy regarding the mythical Greyhound, a man who will save Italy and take it into another age. I knew from my reading that scholars have often speculated that Dante was referring to Cangrande — but what if he meant someone else?

Here I was faced with a decision: *Can I bring the prophecies of Shakespeare and Dante together, roll them together, and slap them on a defenseless child still in his crib? Am I that cruel?*

Turns out I am. Researching astrology and numerology, I came up with a prophetic doom revolving around Dante's Greyhound that all my characters could struggle against in vain. With the advantage of hindsight, I can say that the 'new age of man' alluded to in the Greyhound prophecy was the Renaissance.

The stars were aligned, and the story poured out. A year for the first draft, then six months for the next, and the next. Once in the thick of it, I started seeing connections with the Bard's other Italian plays. Characters and events from *The Taming of the Shrew* are actually mentioned in R&J, so Kate and Petruchio make cameo appearances. There are also characters from *Two Gentlemen of Verona*, of course, but others, as well — Shylock, Don Pedro of Aragon, and his nasty bastard brother. The Duke from *Measure for Measure* (also an Escalus) is mentioned in passing. And what Italian story can miss references to Caesar and Cleopatra? The original idea of the Capulet-Montague feud had blossomed into a panoramic story about Shakespeare's characters living in Dante's world.

Thus was born *The Master of Verona* (2007) and its sequels, *Voice of the Falconer* (2012), *Fortune's Fool* (2012), *The Prince's Doom* (2013), and *Varnished Faces* (2015).

The *Star-Cross'd* series.

I've read that when Alan Alda met Donald Sutherland, he simply took the other man's hand and said, "Thank you for my life." If Shakespeare were alive today, I'm sure that's what I'd have to say.

But I'd start by telling him how I'd always hated him.

Origin of the Feud

In the ramp-up to my first time directing R&J, I was reading and re-reading the script, watching other productions, and even visiting Verona as a lark — not that Shakespeare ever went there, but for the past hundred years or so, the city has become, at least partially, an industry town for the play. Shakespeare's Italian Disneyland.

Used to looking at a play through the eyes of a single character, this was the first time since Mr. Tobin's ninth-grade English class that I was forced to explore the play as a whole. I took a look at all the questions, including the perennial, 'What caused the feud?' Not technically vital to either an actor's or audience's understanding of the show because, at the top of Act One, the feud is an established fact. But still, worth pondering.

Cutting a script is still my least favorite chore. Back then, it drove me mad. What to keep, what to lose? I was nearly done, working on the final scene — Paris is slain, Romeo and Juliet are both dead, we're firmly into the denouement — when suddenly a line jumped out at me.

Capulet and his wife have just found their daughter's bleeding body. Romeo's father, Lord Montague, enters, and the Prince addresses him:

> *Come, Montague, for thou art early up*
> *To see thy son and heir now early down.*

Montague replies:

> *Alas, my liege, my wife is dead tonight;*
> *Grief of my son's exile hath stopped her breath.*
> *What further woe conspires against my age?*

These lines baffled me. Realize, I'd been looking at the show for days, thinking about actors entering and exiting, considering who I could double-cast, and so forth. I clearly didn't need Lady Montague for the final scene — her husband just told us she's dead. I flipped back to find her last scene. She's listed as entering in Act Three, Scene Four, when Mercutio and Tybalt both buy it — but she's strangely quiet in that scene. Lord Capulet, too, but at least people talk to him. No one addresses Romeo's mom, even when her son is banished. In fact, looking at it harder, Lady Montague hasn't been heard from since Act One, Scene One, in which she utters a mere two lines!

So this was my quandary — do I cut Montague's lines at the end of the show? Why not? Here we are, the play is basically over. We've just watched the two romantic leads die pitiably, and young, kind, noble Paris croaks, as well. Why do we care if some woman we barely remember is dead?

But it continued to bother me. There had to be a reason she was dead.

Of course, in Shakespeare's day, there was a very good reason. The actor who played Lady Montague was probably needed in another role — the exigencies of the stage. Even realizing this, though, I couldn't let go of the line. *My wife is dead tonight.* The rules of dramatic structure nagged at me. A death like that is supposed to be symbolic. But of what? Clueless, I shrugged and finished the cuts. I left the line in, hoping my actors could figure it out.

In the event, they didn't have to. I was going about my business later that week when it hit me — *the Feud!* The thing that gets closure at the end of the show is the feud. Montague and Capulet bury the hatchet. They're even going to build statues to honor their dead kids.

> Could Lady Montague's death be symbolic of the end of the feud? The only way that could work would be…

If she were the cause of the feud.

I remember stopping dead in my tracks as the idea took form: a love triangle a generation earlier, between the parents! Romeo's mother, engaged to a young Capulet, runs off with a young Montague instead. That's certainly cause for a feud, especially if young Capulet and Montague were friends. Best friends, childhood friends, torn apart by their love for a woman.

This explained so much in the play — Lord Capulet, Juliet's doting father, suddenly threatening to kill her for refusing to marry the man he's chosen for her. He tells her to "hang, beg, starve, die in the streets" — this from a man who has called her "the hopeful lady of my earth." His fury seems to come out of nowhere and is brutally excessive. But if his own bride-to-be had jilted him and run off with his best friend instead, of course Juliet's similar behavior would press his buttons.

This notion also goes on to inform much of Capulet's relationship with his wife — a younger wife, we know from the script, not well contented in her match, married to a man who doesn't love her. It hints at her relationship, in turn, with Tybalt. In fact, the behavior of both families is wonderfully colored by this single, simple idea: Romeo's mom jilted Juliet's dad. Whoa.

This idea doesn't interfere the actual performance of the show. The reason we are still doing Shakespeare four hundred years later is not his plots, which are stolen and often dippy. It's his language. And *Romeo and Juliet* stands, as it always has, on its language and its near-perfect structure. Any back-story ends up being superfluous.

Yes, there are moments when it can be very clear, but contrary to popular opinion, the core of the play isn't the feud. That's what frustrates me when I see people set the play between rival ethnic groups and think they're making a statement. The feud is simply the setting, the circumstance. It's not the heart of the show.

The heart of the show is youthful love, which is doomed because it burns so hot. Which is why I like this origin to the feud.

A feud born of love, dies with love.

Sources

Tracing the sources of Shakespeare's plays to their roots is fun, though sometimes vexing. Do you work backwards, or try to trace the evolution from ancient texts to his eventual recreation?

Chronologically, the most obvious inspiration for this tale is Ovid's *Metamorphoses*, which includes the tragic tale of Pyramus and Thisbe, a story Shakespeare clearly knew well. So well, in fact, he parodied his own success with R&J by having Bottom and the Mechanicals (a band name if I ever heard one) utterly butcher the source material.

(Aside: Shakespeare was hilariously self-referential in subtle ways. He let us know how he felt about contemporary productions of his works and the actors who played in them, peppering his work with inside jokes. Hamlet's advice to the players is too spot-on, his ridicule of Bottom's scenery-chewing too knowing. He had to be making fun of his fellows – and himself.)

The next relative of this story is certainly a distant one: the *Ephesiaca* of Xenophon of Ephesus, written in the fifth century CE. The lovers Anthia and Habrocomes are on their way to Egypt when they are taken by pirates. Sold into slavery, they are separated, undergoing several rather lusty adventures. At one point Anthia is shipwrecked with her new owners and kidnapped by robbers. She's about to be sacrificed to Ares when she's rescued by a local magistrate called Periaus, who declares his right to marry her. Faithful to her husband, she obtains a potion from a doctor which she thinks is lethal but (as in *Cymbeline*) is merely a sleeping potion. She awakens in a tomb and, due to the consistency of her luck, is carried off by tomb-robbers to further adventures (it totally gives off that *Perils of Pauline* vibe).

Leaping ahead nearly a thousand years, we reach the first of the stories recognizable as direct antecedents of R&J: Masuccio Salernitano's thirty-third novel from *Il Novellino*. Set in Sienna, this work stars Mariotto and Gianozza as the lovers and involves secret marriages, deaths of kinsmen, and a young groom fleeing to Alexandria. The bride is then forced to marry against her will, but is given a draught by the Friar that makes her appear dead. Alas, the Friar's message detailing the plan is waylaid by pirates (shades of *Shakespeare in Love*!). The story plays out the same as R&J, except Gianozza flees to a convent, where she dies. Pregnant, if I recall correctly.

Next comes the first version to name the lovers Romeo and Giulietta in probably the most important of Shakespeare's sources (though he himself may never have seen it). This was written by Luigi da Porto somewhere around 1524, though published posthumously in 1535.

A native of Vicenza, da Porto set the action in nearby Verona, rooting the story very firmly in the reign of Bartolomeo della Scala, 1301-1304. He dedicated his story to "the most beautiful and graceful Lady Lucina Savorgnano." This version is completely recognizable, starting with the establishment of the Cappelletti-Montecchi feud. Romeo Montecchio goes to the Cappelletti ball to see one lady, but upon sight of Giulietta Cappelletti, he falls madly in love. She does the same, and while she's dancing he holds one of her hands (her other hand is held by a suitor named Maruccio who, we are told, is noble and handsome. But she doesn't like him because "in July and in January, his hands were always freezing.").

The two begin to meet in secret, "sometimes in the church, at others from the windows." Then we get the Balcony Scene, with these lines:

GIULIETTA:
What brings you hither and alone at this hour?

ROMEO:
The power of love.

GIULIETTA:
And know you not that being discovered here would mean instantaneous death?

ROMEO:
Alas, dear lady, I know only too well, and certain it is I shall surely die unless you take pity on me. But, as I must die in some place, Heaven grant that I may die near you, who are the goddess of my idolatry and with whom life would seem paradise, would you and Heaven only consent to give ear to my love.

Enlisting the aid of Friar Lorenzo, Giulietta's confessor, they wed in secret. But there's a brawl in the street between the feuding families, and in the massive fighting, Romeo kills Tebaldo Cappelletto. Exiled, Romeo says farewell to his wife in the friar's confessional, then flees to Mantua.

Lord and Lady Cappelletti, misconstruing their daughter's distress, decide to marry her to the cold-handed Maruccio. Hearing her absolute refusal, her father loses his temper and "threatened her with his bitterest hatred if she dared oppose his wishes." Desperate, Giulietta sends her servant Pietro to Romeo in Mantua. Romeo sends word back that she must be faithful to him, and instructs her to go to the friar, as the holy man "was capable of working miracles."

She does, and Lorenzo gives her a potion "which you will drink, after which you will, for a space for forty-eight hours, more or less, fall into a profound sleep that no man, however great a physician he may be, cannot choose but pronounce you dead." He'll be there when she wakes and conduct her to her husband in Mantua.

It plays out just the same. She takes the potion and is thought dead. But the monk Lorenzo sent to Romeo can't find him. Instead, the faithful Pietro brings the news of her death to Romeo, who buys a poison and goes back to Verona, blaming himself:

ROMEO:
I am the sole cause of thy death, for I kept not my promise to take thee away from thy father's house, and thou, who would not forsake me, preferred to die. Should I, through fear of death, remain alive? No, this shall never be.

He goes to her tomb and drinks the poison. Just then, she wakes up, and he bitterly laments, "Oh, how cruel is fate!" He tells her what he has done, and the weeping Giulietta kisses him, "imprinting innumerable kiss on his lips."

GIULIETTA:
Must you die in my presence and for my sake, my sweet lord? Will the Heavens suffer that after your death I should live even for a brief while? Cannot I give you my life and die alone?

ROMEO:
If ever my love and fidelity were dear to you, live, if only for my sake. I therefore beg of you that after my life you continue to live, for no other reason than I may know that one I so dearly love is thinking of me, who is now dying before your very eyes.

GIULIETTA:
Since you die on account of my feigned death, what should I do for your real one? I grieve also that I have not here at hand any means whereby I can die and hate myself that I must still continue to live, but I fervently pray that in a brief time, since I have been the cause of your death, I may bear you company.

Friar Lorenzo arrives just in time to see Romeo die in Giulietta's arms. He says, "And you, Giulietta, what will you do now?"

GIULIETTA
Remain here and die.

Which bring us to the worst death in literature: "Then, holding her breath for a long time, she uttered forth a piercing scream, falling stone dead upon the body of her husband." Because that works?

Everyone comes rushing in, the friar confesses, and the bereaved parents embrace, burying the feud, and raise a monument to their lost children.

"Here finished the unfortunate love affair of Romeo Montecchi and Giulietta Cappelletti."

In 1542, a Frenchman named Adrian Sevin also riffed on the work of Masuccio Salernitano, changing the names to Halquadrich and Burglipha. And a poem by Clizia was published in Venice in 1553.

But the direct heir to da Porto is Matteo Bandello, who basically rewrote da Porto's version, only adding the name Paris to the story, and changing the name Maruccio to Marcuccio — one step closer to Mercutio.

Bandello's minor changes notwithstanding, he's significant because he left Italy toward the end of his life, bringing the story of Romeo and Giulietta to France, and thus closer to England. His version was so popular it was picked up in Venice by the blind poet and playwright Luigi Groto, the first to turn it into a play, published in Italian in 1578. In the play, a nightingale sings when the lovers are to part.

Bandello's version was also picked up by a French poet named Pierre Boaistuau, who rewrote the whole thing in his native tongue, making subtle changes — instead of going to the Capulet ball to forget his puppy love, Romeo goes in hopes of seeing her; he obtains the potion from an avaricious apothecary; and Romeo dies before Juliet awakens, thus omitting what is (to me) the best scene in the story, a mistake that Shakespeare will repeat.

Boaistuau was translated into English by William Painter in his collection of tales entitled *Palace of Pleasure*, published in 1567. But before that, in 1562, Boaistuau's version was brought into the English tongue, retold and embellished by one Arthur Brooke in *The Tragicall Historye of Romeus and Juliet*. By now, the story is fairly well in place, and though I find Brooke almost unreadable, his version was very popular during Elizabeth's reign, reprinted in 1582 and again in 1587. It was even imitated in Bernard Garter's *Two English Lovers*, which, as the title indicates, transfers the setting to England.

It is almost certainly from Brooke's poem that Shakespeare took his inspiration. It's possible he also read Painter's version, but in Brooke's, he has everything he needs to fire his imagination and create the play we know. Everything, that is, save great poetry. Shakespeare performs an amazing piece of alchemy, taking a leaden and dull narrative and turning it into gold.

Thus we have the progression in the evolution of *Romeo and Juliet* — da Porto to Bandello to Brooke to Shakespeare, with various off-shoots along the way. Convoluted? Perhaps. But fascinating, and well worth the roundabout journey.

Now we reach the play itself.

The first legitimate publication of Shakespeare's plays was the *First Folio*, generally considered to be the Holy Grail of Shakespeare texts. Put together by his actors in a wonderfully mercenary attempt to raise cash after he died ("Dammit, if Ben Johnson can make a fortune selling his damn skits, we'd best get in on that!"), it sets down in print together for the first time the Bard's most famous plays.

But there are discrepancies. Because of the expense involved in copying out a play, only the prompter or stage manager would have had a full text. Actors had their cues, their lines, and their stage directions, usually worked into the text. So when Condell and Heminges tried to put together thirty-six plays, there were several missing. Some they reconstructed by memory, or got lucky and the actors had held onto their rolls of ink-stained parchment (where we get the word "role"). For some, they had complete texts, thanks to a fastidious stage manager.

And some were taken from the Quartos.

In publishing terms, a Quarto is the result when four leaves of a book are created from a standard size sheet of paper. Each leaf is usually printed on both sides, leaving eight printed pages in total. In Shakespeare's, time this was true, but there was another wonderful connotation — bootleg.

Today, when a movie comes out, there are always some jerks in the audience with video cameras, and a shaky version of the film shows up the next day on the internet. This happened during Shakespeare's heyday, too. Pretend you're an Elizabethan going to see, say, *Measure for Measure*. You're rich, so you've got a seat in the balcony. Down the row from you, some shifty-looking patron is sitting with a quill and ink-pot, scribbling in a fast shorthand every word the actors below are saying. A week later, you see advertised at a different theatre a play called, astonishingly, *Measure for Measure*. There are no copyright laws, no redress or remuneration for the playwright. That's just the way it goes.

Sometimes a Quarto would be published by the author himself, but far more often a Quarto of some play would appear having been "stolen," as it were, from a live performance. These Quartos sometimes have wild differences from the Folio versions, as bootleggers often could not write as fast as actors spoke. There were gaps that had to be filled in. If there are lots of these gaps, caulked in with low verse and poor rhymes, you get what is known as a 'Bad' Quarto.

Which was how the first printed edition of the play was published by John Danter in 1597. This is known as the Bad Quarto, or "Eeeevil" Quarto because there are so many discrepancies between this and the other versions we have.

What's wrong with the Bad Quarto? Well, it's chock full of what you would expect from a bootleg version of a play — transpositions, paraphrases, summaries, repetitions, and omissions of words, phrases, or lines. But there's a lot in there that we recognize — sometimes more than in the 'Good' Quarto.

That second, the Good Quarto, was released by Thomas Crede for Cuthbert Burby in 1599. It straight up says it has been "Newly corrected, augmented and amended." About 800 lines longer than the Bad Quarto, it's basically the version that all others are taken from, including the Folio. Yet it has some strange mistakes in it, such as Romeo dying twice. Some therefore think it wasn't taken from a clean prompter's copy, but rather from Shakespeare's own "Foul Papers", the crossed-out and revised pages written by the playwright himself.

The text we read today is always a conflation of the two. Why? Because the Bad Quarto has some far more elegant turns of phrase than the Good one. For example, the Good Quarto (usually referred to as Q2) has Romeo say, "I denie you starres!" Whereas the Bad Quarto (Q1) has him say, "I defie you Starres!" To my mind, the latter is by far the stronger choice, and generations of editors agree (my wife and a bevy of Romeo actors do not).

Thus the task of creating a script for any production of R&J falls to the director, cutting and moving and choosing words and paragraphs from different versions. I say this because too often we think there is a "correct" version. We have our Riverside or our Penguin edition or our Arden, and we stop there. But those texts have all been massaged by editors to fit their views of what the play is. Spelling has been altered, punctuation moved, words substituted. Directors and actors should scour all the available choices so that the play best reflects their own vision of the show.

You know it's what Shakespeare would have done.

Don't Believe the Title

I venture into the realm of the painfully obvious when I say that, since it was first penned somewhere around 1595, Shakespeare's *Romeo and Juliet* has become timeless. As an actor, it's been my good fortune to perform most of the male roles in the show — Romeo, Tybalt, Lord Capulet, the Friar, Lord Montague. But the role I've been called back to most often, the first part I ever took up, is Mercutio. It was through his eyes that I first started to understand the play as a whole. And over time and many, many productions, I began to think that all the various directors, with all due respect, had missed the boat.

Because *The Tragedy of Romeo and Juliet* is not a Tragedy at all.

A Shakespearean Tragedy (or Aristotelian, if you're being picky) revolves around a single strong central male figure who is a paragon of virtues, the best at everything a man can be — lover, poet, politician, warrior, philosopher—but who has one tragic flaw that leads to his ultimate destruction. With Macbeth it's Ambition, with Othello it's Jealousy, and so on.

That definition doesn't apply to the leading man in R&J. At the start of the show, Romeo's locking himself in a dark room during the day, then wandering the edge of the forest at night, composing love odes to Rosaline, who is going to become a nun.

Romeo is a prat.

A million years ago, I was in rehearsals for a production of *As You Like It*, watching Orlando running around the forest posting those god-awful poems to Rosalind when I suddenly realized, *Oh. It's Romeo.*

Fortunately for us all, Romeo is much cleverer than Orlando, but the core character is the same. Romeo is not Hamlet or Macbeth or Othello. He's Orlando, Claudio, Orsino. He's a Comedic lover.

Suddenly I started thinking of all the elements of a Shakespearean Comedy. I'm of the opinion the best of his Comedies is *Twelfth Night*. It has everything: lovesick man loving the wrong woman only to discover true love; smart, capable young woman in dire circumstances; clowns; disguises; musicians; mis-timings; twins; shipwrecks; and a woman disguised as a man.

So I began comparing that list to R&J:

Lovesick fool — Romeo. Check.

Capable girl in dire circumstance — Juliet. Check.

Clowns — Mercutio, Nurse, Peter, Potpan, etc. Check.

Disguises — masked ball (though it's only the boys who are crashing who show up in masks! It's not a costume party, damn it!). Check.

Musicians — the often cut but truly funny musicians who are present for the discovery of "dead" Juliet. Check.

Mis-timings — Tybalt kills Mercutio by accident, Friar Lawrence's message misses Romeo, Romeo kills himself just before Juliet wakes, etc. Check.

Secret wedding — Check.

Looking at that list, I realized that the only things this Comedy lacks are twins, shipwrecks, and Juliet dressing as a man. In fact, the very same plan the Friar employs in *Much Ado About Nothing* ("Let's pretend she's dead, and everything will be okay,") is used in R&J — except here it doesn't work.

Oh, and R&J is missing one more element of a Comedy. A happy ending.

So *Romeo and Juliet* is not a Tragedy.

It's a Comedy gone horribly wrong.

When I talk about *Romeo and Juliet*, I like to compare it to the premiere of Walt Disney's *Snow White and the Seven Dwarves* in 1937.

Bear with me here.

Before the film was released, the newspapers called it "Disney's Folly." Walt was spending all his hard-earned Mickey Mouse money on a feature-length cartoon? Why? No one would sit through something like that. Kids didn't have the patience, and adults didn't care about dancing trees or whatever hokum he was putting in it. Besides, all that color on the screen, you'd go blind!

But in December 1937, grown men and women left the premiere of the film weeping. The critics went nuts with praise. Every song became a top-ten hit. Fashion designers grew obsessed (Lucile Ball went to the Oscars that year in a Dopey hat). And theatre owners were forced to change seat covers after every showing because of kids wetting themselves in terror and delight.

Why? Because no one had ever seen anything like it.

That's what I think *Romeo and Juliet* was for the mid-1590s. The first half of the show is a typical Shakespearean Comedy, complete with sex jokes and idiot lovers. The show is funny. I mean, really funny. Read right, the balcony scene has a lot of truly comic elements.

In a normal Comedy, like say *Shrew*, everything is revealed right after the secret wedding and everyone lives happily ever after. Here, however, the wedding is followed by the death of Mercutio, sending the play into a spiral to Hell.

The characters become trapped in an awful situation, trying to find a Comedic solution that isn't there. It's why the Nurse betrays Juliet's trust. It's why Capulet insists on a wedding. It's not a mistake that the Friar's plan is the exact same one that Friar Francis uses in *Much Ado*. It just goes horribly wrong.

At the center of this play is an oddball, the character who twists everything around and turns the play on its head: Mercutio, kinsman to the Prince. The best role Shakespeare ever wrote for a young man. All the best lines, a great psychedelic speech, a bawdy chase, a cool fight, and an angry death, then backstage to drink and play cards until curtain-call.

His Queen Mab speech is a clue. Like the play, Mab starts out nice and airy and fun. Then in the middle, for no reason at all, it twists and becomes dark, the imagery grotesquely foreboding. It's no coincidence that this speech is delivered by the person whose death will cause the same dark turn in the play.

Today we all know the story. But 400 years ago, no one had ever seen anything like it. Shakespeare ripped the rug out from underneath his audience.

Romeo and Juliet is not a Tragedy. It is something much worse.

Because first it makes you laugh.

The Prologue

I never enjoy productions of *Romeo and Juliet* that play the Tragedy from the beginning — probably because I don't think it is a Tragedy at all (see above). But even if it were, this isn't *Hamlet* or *Macbeth*. There's no ghost, no witch. The first half of the show is really, really funny. If you play the Tragic elements of the show from the get-go, the show becomes a dirge. Whereas if you play it as written, as an Italian Comedy, it moves right along.

Wait, you ask. *What about the Prologue?*
Screw the Prologue, say I.

I don't care how famous it is, the Prologue feels tacked on. After all, it doesn't appear in the *First Folio* of 1623. Yes, it does appear in the two Bad Quartos of 1597 and 1599, so it certainly existed. But the Folio version begins with two guys walking down the street talking about sex and violence: "I will push Montague's men from the wall, and thrust his maids to the wall." That's a vibrant and hilarious opening. Starting with the Prologue only serves to make the audience brace themselves, hunker down, hold themselves in emotional reserve.

Read the Prologue again:

> *Two households, both alike in dignity,*
> *In fair Verona, where we lay our scene,*
> *From ancient grudge break to new mutiny,*

Where civil blood makes civil hands unclean.
From forth the fatal loins of these two foes
A pair of star-cross'd lovers take their life;
Whose misadventured piteous overthrows
Do with their death bury their parents' strife.
The fearful passage of their death-mark'd love,
And the continuance of their parents' rage,
Which, but their children's end, nought could remove,
Is now the two hours' traffic of our stage;
The which if you with patient ears attend,
What here shall miss, our toil shall strive to mend.

What the hell? Seriously, what the hell? Telling everyone at the top what the end is going to be? No self-respecting playwright would do such a thing! Shakespeare was a big believer in the old maxim "Show, Don't Tell." He liked Roman theatre, not Greek.

Moreover, it can't be there to explain the feud, because that's explored right off the bat by Sampson and Gregory. It can't be there to establish the location, because the Prince says Verona several times in his opening speech.

No, the only vital purpose the Prologue serves is as a disclaimer, a warning: *Don't laugh too much, folks, because they're gonna die. See you at the end!*

Shakespeare didn't think much of prologues. The only other times he used them was in *Troilus and Cressida*, where he was aping the Greek style, and in *Henry V*, where he was making a political statement at the top of each act.

Why use one in R&J, then? Because this show could have gotten him lynched by an angry mob.

Imagine if the disclaimer wasn't there. The audience is laughing at the Nurse, smiling at the familiar banter of the lovers, enjoying the light-hearted swordplay. Then, snap, someone's dead. Then another person is dead, followed by weeping and wailing and gnashing of teeth. Then, oh look, she's faking her death just like Hero in *Much Ado*, they're going to be fine — wait, what, they're dead?!

Thus the Prologue is a warning to the audience to keep the players from being beaten to death after the show by an angry mob.

The author of the Prologue even felt the need to repeat it! Just before the balcony scene, the Prologue returns to remind everyone:

> *Now old desire doth in his death-bed lie,*
> *And young affection gapes to be his heir;*
> *That fair for which love groan'd for and would die,*
> *With tender Juliet match'd, is now not fair.*
> *Now Romeo is beloved and loves again,*
> *Alike bewitched by the charm of looks,*
> *But to his foe supposed he must complain,*
> *And she steal love's sweet bait from fearful hooks:*
> *Being held a foe, he may not have access*
> *To breathe such vows as lovers use to swear;*
> *And she as much in love, her means much less*
> *To meet her new-beloved any where:*
> *But passion lends them power, time means, to meet*
> *Tempering extremities with extreme sweet.*

Death-bed? Gapes? Bewitched? Not the most romantic of language. "Glad you're enjoying the show, folks, but they're still gonna snuff it! Enjoy watching them hook up, and see you at the end!"

All this explains why, whenever called upon to direct the show, I cut the Prologue. It serves no useful purpose, gives no information we don't get elsewhere, and undercuts the power of the story right out the gate.

The Real Capulets & Montagues of Verona

Someone once found my website by Googling the names Antonio Capulletto and Mariotto Montecchio. It's flattering, as the only way that person could have gotten those names is by reading my novel.

Because I made them up.

With that in mind, I feel honor-bound to make clear a bit about names and history.

There were real Montagues and Capulets. They were actual families — Montecchi e Cappelletti. Dante is the most famous person to mention them (*Purgatorio*, Canto VI), but they are in many histories and period chronicles, as well.

They didn't feud much in Verona, actually. Their clashes were better chronicled happening around Cremona. My only guess as to why so many writers connected them with Verona is that there is a castle and a village between Verona and Vicenza called Montecchio.

Most often, period Italian names indicate the place of origin, not the place of current residence. If I was born in Parma but lived in Venice, I would be David of Parma. Everybody would know who that was. Then, after a few generations, the name is still there. My son would be Dash of Parma, even though he'd never been to Parma in his life.

Now, there were Montecchi who were intimately involved in Veronese affairs — but that wasn't the branch of the family famous for feuding. It's more likely that the Montecchi in Cremona originally came from the village of Montecchio, and were neither the owners of that castle nor the masters of that village.

The first mention of the Montecchi comes in a document dated 1136, which lists Giovanni Monticulo, whose brother Gomberto is mentioned in 1157, and whose son Giacomo is listed in 1177. Giacomo's son is mentioned in 1206.

But the Montecchi seem to have died out as a family, the name being taken on more as a political faction in and around Verona.

The Cappelletti seem to have had the exact opposite genesis. They first appear in Cremona as a political faction, not an actual family — they evidently marked themselves by wearing little hats, hence the name. Exiled from Cremona in 1249, they were not allowed to return until 1267. Perhaps that's when some of the Cappelletti settled in Verona. Only in 1427 do we see the name applied to a family.

By the time the play was written, most of the Capulets and Montagues around Verona had died off or moved away.

Which is where things get weird.

In 1575 in England, there was a double wedding. The son of Viscount Montacute and the daughter of Sir William Dormer were to wed, and Montacute's daughter was promised to Sir William's son. It was a grand affair, and they "determined to present a Maske, and so farre they had proceeded therein, that they had already bought furniture of Silkes, &c, and had caused their garmentes to bee cut of the Venetian fashion." For the Maske, they commissioned the poet George Gascoigne to construct a play to explain the Venetian dress. Familiar with Brooke's poem, Gascoigne made the natural leap of connecting the Montacutes of England to the Montagues (as it was in

French) of Verona. But he went further, crafting an incredible history of the last of the Italian Montagues. "His father being slaine at the lawarres against the Turke, and he there taken, hee was recovered by the Venetians in their last victorie, andith them sayling towardes Venice, they were driven by tempest upon these coastes, and so came to the marriage upon report as followeth…" It's both preposterous and lovely—and just the kind of thing that might spark someone to write a novel…

But not today.

Interestingly, Shakespeare gives the Prince the name Escalus. Or at least the script does, as it's a name that's never once spoken in the text. But in the Dramatis Personae, he's Escalus, Prince of Verona.

That's fascinating, because it lines up with the real princes of Verona in the late thirteenth and early fourteenth centuries. The family was called della Scala, meaning "of the ladder." Their crest was even a ladder.

Doubtless Shakespeare cribbed the name from Arthur Brooke's poem, from whence he also purloined Mercutio. But it's interesting that the historical family should survive in name in the play.

Luigi da Porto's version of the play says the events of R&J took place during the time of Bartolomeo della Scala. Bartolomeo was well-liked, but far from extraordinary. It's his little brother who became a legend in his own lifetime. Cangrande della Scala, the "great hound" of Verona, who conquered the whole of the Trevisian Mark, only to be poisoned on the eve of his greatest victory. Dante dedicated his *Paradiso* to Cangrande, and he is remembered even today in Verona — everywhere one turns, there's the ladder crest.

I did a lot of research into Cangrande, and he became so important to my novel that the book ended up being titled for him.

He was the perfect figure for a Shakespearean tragedy, the best at everything a man should be, but with a tragic flaw that led to his destruction right at the height of his power.

However, by my timeline, it's not Cangrande but his nephew Mastino who rules Verona at the time of R&J. Poetically, it makes much more sense. Mastino was an ineffectual ruler, both at home and abroad. Under him, Verona lost all the lands Cangrande had gained. So if the flowers of Verona's youth are all to die in some godawful love feud, it fits perfectly the trajectory of Mastino's reign.

Draw Thy Tool

I am eternally surprised that *Romeo and Juliet* is the play we teach in high schools.

On one level, it's perfectly natural. After all, the leads are teens (well, Juliet is. We hope Romeo is, as well, though his age is never actually stated). Students are meant to see themselves in them and their friends, and the familiarity is meant to provide a door into Shakespeare's language and world.

Don't get me wrong, I think that's spot-on. One of Shakespeare's gifts is fully inhabiting his characters. A doting father feels as authentic as a rebellious daughter, and a tired old priest is no more real than a lovesick teen. I also think R&J, as a whole, is perfectly structured, and therefore a great introduction to the five-act play. Nevertheless, I'm always a little shocked to hear high-schoolers are reading it.

So often after a student matinee, a teacher or parent will complain, "Why did you add all those sex jokes?" When we say we didn't add them, they assure us we did. "I know *Romeo and Juliet*, and that's not in there!" When we take them through the script line by line, they're shocked and proceed to tell us we shouldn't have performed it the way Shakespeare wrote it.

I guess it's important that our students read Shakespeare, just so long as they don't understand it.

Because it is the filthiest play in the canon.

Being true to his young male characters, Shakespeare has them engage in the Elizabethan equivalent of "locker room talk" (a term that today feels as gross as it always should have). Double-entendres? They abound. Hell, the play begins with two servants talking sex and death. "I will push Montague's men from the wall, and thrust his Maides to the wall." The first page of the text is rife with "me they shall feel," "pretty piece of flesh," "draw thy tool," and maidenhead jokes. Out of the gate, this is filthy.

It hardly improves when the nobility arrives. Benvolio is quite respectful and poetic when talking to his aunt and uncle. But the moment his cousin Romeo appears, he's all, "A right faire marke, faire Coz, is soonest hit." Hell, even lovelorn Romeo says that the object of his affection will not "open her lap to Saint-seducing Gold." What, did Romeo try to bribe her to sleep with him?

The entire conversation about Rosalind is Romeo's lament that she won't sleep with him:

BENVOLIO:
Then she hath sworne, that she will still liue chaste?

ROMEO:
She hath, and in that sparing make huge waste!

But it's not only the boys. No, the ladies also have the chance to be filthy. We start with the Nurse, who tells a story so hilariously ribald that she has to repeat it three times because she can't stop laughing: "Oh Juliet, when you were little you fell on your face, and my husband picked you up and said, 'When you're older, you'll fall on your back, won't you?' And you said, 'Yeah!'"

Lecturing a high-school class once, I mentioned this joke, and the students all looked at me blankly. "That's not in there," they said.

"Of course it is," I answered, confidently opening their textbook. Imagine my chagrin to find that speech entirely omitted from the text! Why are you reading bowdlerized Shakespeare? I mean, you can get away with cutting the dirty jokes from, say, *Julius Caesar,* because there really aren't any. But *Romeo and Juliet* is one-third romance, one-third sword-fighting, and one-third penis jokes.

Once I was part of a company doing Shakespeare for high-school students. After one of our performances, we got threats of picketing. Why? Because some woman's son (who hadn't seen the play) was talking to a friend (who had) and was told the Nurse had grabbed her own breast on the line 'for I had then laid Worme-wood to my Dug sitting in the Sunne under the Douehouse wall.' Okay, a cheap laugh, but it's a line about breastfeeding, not sex (a rare exception in this show). Yet this was considered so scandalous that it ended up in the newspapers that we were doing pornographic Shakespeare!

(The delightful part of that episode was the woman giving the newspaper the quote, "I've read *Romeo and Juliet*, and that's not in there." The entire comments section of the article was filled with readers quoting all the dirty lines from the play at her. The threat of picketing vanished as she quickly realized she had no idea what she was talking about.)

Romeo and Juliet is possibly Shakespeare's dirtiest play, which makes total sense, being about teenagers. But once again, people have this grand romantic ideal of it that has nothing at all to do with the play itself.

Notice, I have not yet mentioned the Ruler of Ribaldry, the Maestro of Immodesty, the Purveyor of Prurience, Mr. Mercutio himself. I close with these lines just before the Balcony Scene:

MERCUTIO:
I conjure thee by Rosalines bright eyes,
By her High forehead, and her Scarlet lip,

> *By her Fine foote, Straight leg, and Quiuering thigh,*
> *And the Demeanes, that there Adjacent lie,*
> *That in thy likenesse thou appeare to vs.*
>
> BENVOLIO:
> *And if he heare thee thou wilt anger him.*
>
> MERCUTIO:
> *This cannot anger him! T'would anger him*
> *To raise a spirit in his Mistresse circle*
> *Of some strange nature, letting it stand*
> *Till she had laid it, and conjured it downe,*
> *That were some spight.*
> *My invocation is faire & honest, & in his Mistris name,*
> *I conjure onely but to raise up him.*

That is one of the most hilariously filthy speeches in Shakespeare. As with everything he does, Mercutio starts out fun, and then descends — in this case, to the domains adjacent to the thigh.

We teach this to high-schoolers. And we should. But I doubt most parents know what it is that's being taught, and poor teachers walk a tightrope of propriety. American culture draws a lot from the Puritans who fled from Shakespeare's England. I have an Australian friend who says, "Thank God we got the convicts and they got the Puritans."

This is exactly the play to hook teens on Shakespeare. So long as they understand it.

The Juliet Trap

There is a very particular trap for actresses playing Juliet. It happens to a lesser extent with Lady Macbeth, and many of the more archetypal male roles. But none of them are as insidious as the Juliet Trap.

Here's how it happens. The good director casts a young woman who auditions with great energy, perfect comedic timing, and no fear of looking bad or awkward. She's attractive, but not so beautiful that it will be awkward — Juliet is thirteen years old, after all.

The actress is thrilled. Juliet is "one of those roles," an ideal and iconic role, a dream role.

And that's where the trap begins to close.

As a society, we all share a collective idea of what Juliet is supposed to be. We envision the party, the balcony, the potion, the tomb. We have this idealized image of youthful, romantic love.

The trouble is, that's not Juliet. At least, it's not the one Shakespeare gives us. On the page she's willful, witty, and wickedly smart. Her only flaw is youth, a lack of experience that makes every moment the most important one in her life. She is, in short, a teenager.

Far too often, no matter how gifted and skilled the actress may be, she stops playing the words on the page. Instead she tries to play the archetype, the ideal version of youthful love.

Which quickly reduces to playing "pretty."

The trouble, of course, is that "pretty" is not an active choice. It's not even a character trait. It's external. It can be achieved with costume and makeup, which all too quickly become the focus.

If you're lucky, the actress only starts speaking softly, with a lilt in her voice and a flip to her hair. You know, "prettily." A good director can nip those in the bud from the jump.

If you're unlucky, she actively tries to be "pretty" and instead comes off as vain, vapid, and shallow. Exactly the opposite of what Juliet should be. She is not a Bianca. She is a Viola.

What lifts the best Juliets from the ranks of the average is losing the fetters of "prettiness" and embracing the comedienne within. Allow her to have awkward teenage moments. Make that first kiss with Romeo an actual first kiss, where they bonk noses. Allow her to prattle and be mortified during the Balcony Scene. Let her be not gracefully in love but ridiculously in love with Romeo.

Because in her exuberant inexperience, we will all recognize our own wonderfully terrible first loves. After all, she is the character we follow in the second half of the play, when things go downhill fast. If we identify with her joy early on, we will suffer all the more as she suffers. Because she will have been made, not ideal, but all too real.

So to all the Juliets out there, remember — play the words on the page. They are so much better than the idealized character in your head.

Speaking of idealizing Juliet, we come now to a strange modern phenomenon. The "Letters to Juliet" world.

I know there are desperate people out there seeking advice on how to live their lives. Dear Abby, Oprah, and Mr. Blue (oh, how I do miss Mr. Blue!) are only a few examples of how authority figures have hundreds, nay, thousands of people seeking their counsel. I have absolutely no issue with this. Everybody needs advice sometimes.

But where you turn for that advice does, in fact, matter.

When she was younger, my wife worked as a receptionist at a television station. Her job was to separate the real calls from the crazies. She was confused by that job description until she fielded a call on her first day from a woman who had burned her hand and wanted to talk to Dr. Quinn, Medicine Woman, for help.

I suppose I have less of a problem with the idea of asking for a fictional character than with the choice of fictional character — wouldn't she rather talk to Dr. Ross or Dr. Carter? Or even the guys from MASH? Someone with a passing knowledge of modern medicine at least? (Not to knock Dr. Quinn — I've met Jane Seymour and she's absolutely lovely. But seriously!)

This, in a roundabout way, brings us to the topic of people writing letters to Juliet. It's been happening for several hundred years. The lovelorn, for the most part, write to her for help. Two authors complied a book of letters written to Juliet in Verona and the answers sent by the club set up just for that purpose. This is the book *Letters to Juliet*, which spawned the film of the same name. Again, kudos.

What I cannot for the life of me fathom is this — why are these people writing to Juliet? Why go to her of all people for help?

There are three distinct problems with their choice of advisor, which I will list in ascending order:

1: She is a fictional character.

2: She's a dead fictional character.

3: Seeing as she's dead because of her love life, why would anyone want her advice in the first place? Her love affair didn't go so well.

Therein lies my frustration with people not thinking through their need for a guide in life. I have less trouble with Linus writing to the Great Pumpkin than I do with people writing to a fictional dead thirteen-year-old.

I mean, really — who asks for love advice from a thirteen-year-old?

Mab

I feel like I should have a lot to say about Mercutio. After all, I've written novels about him. Until recent years, he was the character I played most often. He ignited my love affair with Shakespeare, and playing him has certainly shaped my life.

Here's the thing about Mercutio — everything you need to know about him exists on the page. The words he speaks, in performance, define his character. Give the words free rein, and the character appears. He's like riding a canoe down a choppy river. Just do your best to hold on and keep from flipping over too often.

There are a few facts that we know. He's the Prince's kinsman and "near ally." He's Romeo's friend, but not a Montague. Based on the references he makes, he's well-educated, yet he has a disdain for anyone who puts on airs, from Romeo to Tybalt to the Nurse. But he's clever, matching Romeo rhyme for rhyme (always the mark of a clever character). He adores wordplay, but isn't above speaking in prose. He's quite sexual in his phraseology, and certainly has a temper. All of which we glean from the text.

Beyond that, there are a few assumptions people make about him — that he's gay, that he's in love with Romeo, that he was based on Kit Marlowe, that he was so interesting that Shakespeare had to kill him off lest he take over the whole play.

As to the first three, which are basically the same, I have no real opinion. There's nothing wrong with playing him gay. He certainly seems to be omnisexual and omnivorous. At the very least he is, to use a 90s phrase, metrosexual. And having him in love with Romeo certainly works. It's not my favorite choice. To me, it undermines a little of his role here — the voice ridiculing love and lovers. If he is an unrequited lover himself, he has much more in common with Romeo than he admits, and his motivation for teasing Romeo out of his love for Rosaline is selfish. But that's a great conflict to play, and certainly there's lots to be made of it.

But it strikes me that, whatever his sexual inclinations at present, Mercutio has loved a woman at least once in his life. And it did not go well.

Why do I think that? Because of the Mab speech.

Much has been made of this speech; certainly it was central to my auditioning life for years. And I don't want to belabor it. Still, before discussing it, here's the speech in its entirety:

ROMEO:
I dreampt a dreame to night.

MERCUTIO:
And so did I.

ROMEO:
Well what was yours?

MERCUTIO:
That dreamers often lye.

ROMEO:
In bed a sleepe while they do dreame things true.

MERCUTIO:

O then I see Queene Mab hath beene with you: She is the Fairies Midwife, & she comes in shape no bigger then Agatstone, on the fore-finger of an Alderman, drawne with a teeme of little Atomies, ouer mens noses as they lie asleepe: her Waggon Spokes made of long Spinners legs: the Couer of the wings of Grashoppers, her Traces of the smallest Spiders web, her coullers of the Moonshines watry Beames, her Whip of Crickets bone, the Lash of Philome, her Waggoner, a small gray-coated Gnat, not halfe so bigge as a round little Worme, prickt from the Lazie-finger of a man. Her Chariot is an emptie Haselnut, made by the Joyner Squirrel or old Grub, time out a mind, the Faries Coach-makers: & in this state she gallops night by night, through Louers braines: and then they dreame of Loue. On Courtiers knees, that dreame on Cursies strait: ore Lawyers fingers, who strait dreamt on Fees, ore Ladies lips, who strait on kisses dreame, which oft the angry Mab with blisters plagues, because their breath with Sweet meats tainted are. Sometime she gallops ore a Courtiers nose, & then dreames he of smelling out a sute: & somtime comes she with Tith pigs tale, tickling a Parsons nose as a lies asleepe, then he dreames of another Benefice. Sometime she driueth ore a Souldiers necke, & then dreames he of cutting Forraine throats, of Breaches, Ambuscados, Spanish Blades: Of Healths fiue Fadome deepe, and then anon drums in his eares, at which he startes and wakes; and being thus frighted, sweares a prayer or two & sleepes againe: this is that very Mab that plats the manes of Horses in the night: & bakes the Elklocks in foule sluttish haires, which once vntangled, muchmisfortune bodes, This is the hag, when Maides lie on their backs, That presses them, and learnes them first to beare, Making them women of good carriage: This is she.

ROMEO:
Peace, peace, Mercutio peace,
Thou talk'st of nothing.

MERCUTIO:
True, I talke of dreames:
Which are the children of an idle braine,
Begot of nothing, but vaine phantasie,
Which is as thin of substance as the ayre,
And more inconstant then the wind, who wooes
Euen now the frozen bosome of the North:
And being anger'd, puffes away from thence,
Turning his side to the dew dropping South.

What do we learn from this? Well, at its most basic, this speech is a classic pair of Shakespeare lists. The first list is of Mab's accoutrements — form, whip, lash, chariot, waggoner, etc. The second list is the types of people that Mab visits in the night, and the kind of dreams she gives them. To begin with, we have a fairly standard list of professions ripe for mockery: Lovers, Courtiers, Lawyers, Ladies, Parsons, Courtiers again.

Then we reach the Soldier. He's notable because he has a two-part prophecy. The first is funny, as he dreams of quite dramatic effects: breaches, ambushes, swords, and drinking.

And then anon drums in his eares, at which he startes and wakes; and being thus frighted, sweares a prayer or two & sleepes againe.

That's different. It's almost reflective, as if Mercutio's cutting outward gaze has turned inward. Melancholy strikes the speech at this point. From this sudden bout of reflection, I imagine Mercutio has been a soldier, or been close to soldiers.

Suddenly, unaccountably, the speech turns quite dark. Suddenly the word "slut" is brought into play, far more judgmental than any term he's used before. Then maids are on their backs and Mab presses them and "learns them how to bear."

Whenever Shakespeare makes a jest involving women and the word "bear," he's talking about both a woman bearing the weight of a man atop her, and pregnancy.

So is the fairy Mab raping women in their dreams? Or delivering them of children? "Women of good carriage" makes me think the latter.

At this point, Romeo stops Mercutio, who tells him he "talkst of nothing."

Mercutio's answer, suddenly in verse, is biting. "True. I talk of dreams."

To the seventeen-year-old me who said these lines without any knowledge of how to interpret them, this was always indicative of some terrible loss, a disillusionment. Combined with his vast disdain for love and lovers, it strikes me that Mercutio loved once. He loved, and now feels betrayed by love.

As readers of my novels will know, I tend to lean toward someone he loves dying in childbirth. It was certainly a common enough occurrence. But perhaps that doesn't account for the betrayal, and the word "slut," so damning. Certainly he has no kind words for any woman, as again and again he condemns them. Yet he knows love poetry well, as we'll see by a quote a couple of chapters further on.

My basic takeaway is that Mercutio disdains Romeo because he was Romeo once, and it did not end well.

But the Queen Mab speech is more than just a window into Mercutio's mind. It's also a piece of the structural perfection of this play, a foreshadowing of the doom to come far more elegant and vibrant than any prologue could ever be. Starting out light and airy, a clown speech that could be in any Shakespearean Comedy. Then, right when it should start wrapping up to a pithy conclusion, it takes a turn and becomes dark and violent, almost pitiable.

Just like the play. Only there is no one to stop the show and shake it from its dark thoughts, urging it back to humor. Instead, it just spirals out of control. That is the legacy of the Mab speech to me. It's a mirror for the show as a whole.

Which brings us to the notion that he was so interesting that Shakespeare had to kill him off. No. Mercutio serves a vital function to the story. He's what throws the Comedy out of joint. It's no accident that the person who gives the Mab speech is also the person whose death leads to the play following in that speech's wake. He's the key domino in the perfect construction of this play. Shakespeare didn't decide to murder him. Shakespeare created him to be murdered.

Huh. Turns out I had stuff to say about Mercutio after all.

It's Not a Masked Ball!

Despite what Baz Luhrmann did in his film, the party in R&J is not a masked ball.

It was common practice in Renaissance Italy to show up wearing a mask to a party one was not invited to. Which is exactly what the boys are doing. Mercutio is even delighted to don a mask to a party he was invited to ("A visor for a visor!").

Why? Because it's much more fun to crash a party than be welcomed.

How do I know it's not a masked ball? Because Capulet makes such a big deal out of the boys showing up masked:

> *Welcome, gentlemen! I have seen the day*
> *That I have worn a visor and could tell*
> *A whispering tale in a fair lady's ear,*
> *Such as would please: 'tis gone, 'tis gone, 'tis gone:*
> *You are welcome, gentlemen!*

Moreover, he remarks how much the boys in masks are going to liven his party, saying, "Ah, sirrah, this unlook'd-for sport comes well." Unlook'd-for being the important phrase here. This was not a party to which everyone was supposed to come masked. It's a large party, and only the crashers are masked.

A few lines later, Capulet asks a relative when the last time they went masked to a party was:

> *Nay, sit, nay, sit, good cousin Capulet;*
> *For you and I are past our dancing days:*
> *How long is't now since last yourself and I*
> *Were in a mask?*

Which brings us to the first of two references to *The Taming of the Shrew*. Second Capulet (sometimes Old Capulet) tells Cap it's been thirty years since they crashed a party in masks. Cap disagrees:

> *What, man! 'tis not so much, 'tis not so much:*
> *'Tis since the nuptial of Lucentio,*
> *Come Pentecost as quickly as it will,*
> *Some five and twenty years; and then we mask'd.*

So Capulet and Old Capulet were at Lucentio and Bianca's wedding (which raises its own problem, seeing as those two were wed in secret…).

At the end of the same scene, as the revelers are departing, the Nurse identifies one of them as "young Petruchio."

Thus we have our timeframe — it's been 25 years since the events of *Shrew*, and Petruchio has a son. It's a lovely in-joke for anyone in Shakespeare's audience who's seen *Shrew* (one that I keep alive in the short story collection *Varnished Faces*).

A final note — the last two times I saw the show, I thought the directors were brilliant (confession: one of them was my wife) in how they handled the Capulet Ball. Because it always feels as though the story has to stop so we can all watch a dance. Whereas these directors put the whole party offstage. The scene we see is on the Capulet yard, or garden, or somewhere just outside the party itself. Man, did that help.

Why? Because Shakespeare parties suck.

In a cast with fifteen men and four women, it's always a sausage-fest. In opera, you have the bodies, but in most Shakespeare productions, you just don't have extra women to put in dresses for that one scene. Which means everyone is looking at Juliet, and Romeo's fascination with her is less impressive — *of course* he notices her, she's the only girl his age onstage!

It also neatly deals with the issue of what to do with the party when Romeo grabs Juliet's hand and begins to talk to her. Do the rest of the revelers freeze? Do they dance in slow-motion? Do the lights dim except for a pin-spot on the lovers as they perform their perfect (and perfectly lovely) sonnet?

No, it makes much more sense that Juliet is escaping the unwanted attentions of Paris by retreating to the garden, where Romeo grasps her hand. It makes the Nurse's line, "Madam, your mother craves a word with you," make much more sense, as she appears from the house where the party continues. Shakespeare loved punctuating onstage action with offstage scenes; the first conversation between Cassius and Brutus in *Caesar* is peppered with shouts and clamors from offstage. Why not here?

In both productions, the choice to move the party offstage got savaged by critics because, once again, people have built up an image of what this show is "supposed to be" rather than what it is. There is no reason for us to see the party, just people going in and out. I cannot tell you how much it helped take the air out of the play, moving it right along.

So, no masks except for the boys, and off-stage dancing. Those are the keys to a good party.

That, and music. Interestingly, there's a piece of music published in 1595 that Shakespeare might have been riffing on. It's a jig-parody of the ballad "Walsingham" and seems particularly apt. Even the song is a dialogue:

BESSIE:
As I went to Walsingham
to the shrine with speed
Met I with a jolly Palmer
in a Pilgrim's weed.
Now God save you jolly Palmer.

FRAUNCIS:
Welcome lady gay,
Of have I sued to thee for love.

BESSIE:
Oft have I said you nay.

This clearly echoes the sonnet of dialogue the lovers have in the party (which I'll discuss in the next section). Oddly, the original song this jig is parodying is the basis for Ophelia's 'How should I your true love know' song.

As you came from Walsingham
from that holy land,
Met you not with my true love
by the way you came?

How should I your true love know,
that hath met many a one,
As I came from the holy land,
that have come, that have gone?...

I like to think Shakespeare's audiences would have caught the allusion.

Redeeming Romeo

Like the Juliet Trap, there is a Romeo Trap. But it is subtly different. It isn't a trap Romeos fall into so much as casting directors. I think they're often looking for the wrong Romeo.

Because there are two Romeos in the show.

The first Romeo, the Romeo we hear about before he ever walks on stage, is the moping Romeo, the sighing Romeo, the pining Romeo. Romeo Stick-in-the-Mud. Romeo in "love."

Only he's not really in love. At the start of the show, Romeo has fallen for the ideal of Romantic Love, of Chivalric Love, of Love from Afar. He loves Rosaline not truly for herself, but because he's enjoying his anguish:

> *Love is a smoke raised with the fume of sighs;*
> *Being purged, a fire sparkling in lovers' eyes;*
> *Being vex'd a sea nourish'd with lovers' tears:*
> *What is it else? a madness most discreet,*
> *A choking gall and a preserving sweet.*

He's not in love with Rosaline. He's in love with *love*. Worse, he's in love with a teenager's idea of being in love — all the *sturm und drang*, none of the calm seas and coming back to harbor.

This was the fashion, starting with the French tales of Lancelot and Guinevere, continuing through Dante's passion for his Beatrice, right through Petrarch's love for his unobtainable Laura. As mentioned before, Mercutio mocks him relentlessly for this:

MERCUTIO:
Alas poor Romeo! he is already dead; stabbed with a white wench's black eye; shot through the ear with a love-song; the very pin of his heart cleft with the blind bow-boy's butt-shaft.

And later:

BENVOLIO:
Here comes Romeo, here comes Romeo.

MERCUTIO:
Without his roe, like a dried herring: flesh, flesh, how art thou fishified! Now is he for the numbers that Petrarch flowed in: Laura to his lady was but a kitchen-wench; marry, she had a better love to be-rhyme her; Dido a dowdy; Cleopatra a gipsy; Helen and Hero hildings and harlots; Thisbe a grey eye or so, but not to the purpose. Signior Romeo, bon jour! there's a French salutation to your French slop.

It's tempting to read "French slop" as a reference to Romeo's mode of attire. But in this case I think Mercutio means this ridiculous notion of Courtly Love, made famous by French poets, where one aspires to love only from afar.

There's a book by Andreas Capellanus entitled *De Amore*, which lists the 31 rules of Courtly Love:

1. Marriage should not be a deterrent to love.

2. Love cannot exist in the individual who cannot be jealous.

3. A double love cannot obligate an individual.

4. Love constantly waxes and wanes.

5. That which is not given freely by the object of one's love loses its savor.

6. It is necessary for a male to reach the age of maturity in order to love.

7. A lover must observe a two-year widowhood after his beloved's death.

8. Only the most urgent circumstances should deprive one of love.

9. Only the insistence of love can motivate one to love.

10. Love cannot coexist with avarice.

11. A lover should not love anyone who would be an embarrassing marriage choice.

12. True love excludes all from its embrace but the beloved.

13. Public revelation of love is deadly to love in most instances.

14. The value of love is commensurate with its difficulty of attainment.

15. The presence of one's beloved causes palpitation of the heart.

16. The sight of one's beloved causes palpitations of the heart.

17. A new love brings an old one to a finish.

18. Good character is the one real requirement for worthiness of love.

19. When love grows faint, its demise is usually certain.

20. Apprehension is the constant companion of true love.

21. Love is reinforced by jealousy.

22. Suspicion of the beloved generates jealousy and therefore intensifies love.

23. Eating and sleeping diminish greatly when one is aggravated by love.

24. The lover's every deed is performed with the thought of his beloved in mind.

25. Unless it please his beloved, no act or thought is worthy to the lover.

26. Love is powerless to hold anything from love.

27. There is no such thing as too much of the pleasure of one's beloved.

28. Presumption on the part of the beloved causes suspicion in the lover.

29. Aggravation of excessive passion does not usually afflict the true lover.

30. Thought of the beloved never leaves the true lover.

31. Two men may love one woman or two women one man.

It's as though Act I Romeo has studied this list, and is determined to stick to it. His friends see this and lament it, missing their witty and joyful friend who has been replaced by this stick-in-the-mud who declares himself incapable of dancing:

> *A torch for me: let wantons light of heart*
> *Tickle the senseless rushes with their heels,*
> *For I am proverb'd with a grandsire phrase;*

I'll be a candle-holder, and look on.
The game was ne'er so fair, and I am done.

Only this is an act. How do we know? The Friar tells us so. When Romeo is complaining that Rosaline never loved him back, Friar Lawrence says:

Oh, she knew well
Thy love did read by rote, that could not spell.

In other words, Rosaline knew that Romeo's love wasn't real. In fact, everybody knew it except Romeo. Certainly Mercutio knows, as he tries to draw his friend "from the mire, or saue your reuerence loue, wherein thou stickest up to the eares."

Though their efforts to tease him out of his "love" failure, Benvolio's plan to make Romeo forget Rosaline succeeds. Because the moment he sees Juliet at the ball, Romeo changes. He throws off the mournful cloak of Courtly Love and suddenly understands what true love is.

Note the exuberance with which Romeo encounters life in Shakespeare's Act Two, after meeting Juliet. He's a different man entirely. His interactions are bright, ebullient, clever, teasing. He's no longer mournful, but bursting with wit. Encountering his friends on the street, his antics move Mercutio to exclaim:

Why is not this better now, then groning for Love,
Now art thou sociable, now art thou Romeo: now art
Thou what thou art, by Art as well as by Nature...

Romeo is himself once more. *This* is Romeo's true nature.

And *this* is the Romeo that casting directors should be looking for. Too often they cast Act One Romeo, when they should be seeking Act Two Romeo. They hire some emo mope who looks great brooding but can't pull off the joy and comedy that Act Two is full of. Once again, we need the comedy of Act Two if we're going to pull the rug out in Act Three.

A lot of people talk about how they hate Romeo. I get it. He makes a lot of rash decisions, and his moping at the top of the show is dreadful. But that's the point. Shakespeare is making a vital distinction between being in love with love, and actual love itself. One, he's telling us, is useless, vain, and wasteful. The other is brilliant and all-intoxicating. Being in love doesn't make you mope. It makes you see the beauty in all things. Romeo is even able to love Tybalt, because he is so happy he can bear any insult given him.

The distinction between Romeo's feelings for Rosaline and those he bears Juliet are often chalked up to him owning a fickle nature. In one sense, I suppose he does. You can certainly find fickleness in the line:

ROMEO:
Did my heart love till now? Forsweare it sight,
For I never saw true Beauty till this night.

Yet there's another way to look at that line. As honest discovery. Make it truthful. Make it wonder-filled. It's like he's shedding an earlier, unworthy version of himself as real love enters his heart. Read that way, he's no longer fickle. He's just growing up. After wanting so very much to feel love, the actual feeling of love is so much more that he forgets all his stupid airs of love and does something unthinkable to a Courtly Lover — he acts! First he grabs the girl by the hand and talks to her, even stealing two kisses.

Much is made of the fact that Romeo and Juliet's first interaction creates a perfect sonnet, leading up to their first kiss.

ROMEO:
If I prophane with my unworthiest hand,
This holy shrine, the gentle sin is this,
My lips two blushing Pilgrims did ready stand,
To smooth that rough touch, with a tender kisse.

JULIET:
Good Pilgrime, you do wrong your hand too much.
Which mannerly deuotion shewes in this,
For Saints have hands, that Pilgrims hands do touch,
And palme to palme, is holy Palmers kisse.

ROMEO:
Have not Saints lips, and holy Palmers too?

JULIET:
Ay, Pilgrim, lips that they must use in prayer.

ROMEO:
O then deare Saint, let lips do what hands do.
They pray. Grant thou, lest faith turne to dispaire.

JULIET:
Saints do not move, though grant for prayers sake.

ROMEO:
Then move not while my prayers effect I take.

Those lines are not only the perfect sonnet's rhyming scheme, but they're also a wonderful bit of clever wordplay. He makes her a saint, she gives him a clever brush-off. He persists, turning her brush-off into a rather ingenious come on ("Let lips do what hands do" – man, that is a truly great line). She demurs, then invites ("Saints do not move..." I won't kiss you. Buuuut I may let you kiss me — if you're honest). He takes her at her word. It goes so well, in fact, she invites him to do it again:

ROMEO:
Thus from my lips, by thine my sin is purg'd.

JULIET:
Then have my lips the sin that they have tooke.

ROMEO:
Sin from my lips? O trespasse sweetly urg'd:
Giue me my sin againe.

JULIET:
You kisse by th'booke.

They even end with a shared line. How romantic is that? (And, if you want to, you can play with her "by the book" line to mean he's still being courtly — and she may be hoping for something less chaste).

Performance note: If you want to model consent, simply put a question mark at the end of Romeo's last line. "Give me my sin again?" is an offer, not a demand or command. In the modern era, where so much of this play comes off as misogynistic and toxic, there is great good to be achieved by having Romeo ask, and Juliet give enthusiastic consent.

If that scene is not proof enough that we have a new Romeo on our hands, in the next scene he is physically unable to leave her home. Instead he leaps her wall in the middle of the night to play Peeping Tom. His love for Rosaline is all talk, whereas his love for Juliet is genuine because it moves him to action!

Which brings us at last to the Balcony Scene. Or, as I like to call it, the Window Scene.

The Window Scene

(OR WE DON'T NEED NO STINKIN' BALCONY)

As you have certainly deduced by now, what drives me crazy about R&J are the number of inane and misguided preconceptions people have about it. There are so many misconceptions about this show, and the biggest of them all is the Balcony Scene. People refer to it as one of the greatest romantic scenes in literature. Hell, the show itself is often called "the greatest love story ever told."

But it's a lie. Because in a great love story, *they'd live.*

Yet the scene itself contains the biggest misconception of them all:

There's no balcony in the Balcony Scene.

Nowhere in the script does it say "balcony." In fact, when Shakespeare wrote the play, the word "balcony" didn't even exist. According to the Oxford English Dictionary, the word "balcony" (then "balcone") made its first appearance in English in the year 1618, two whole years after Shakespeare's death and twenty-odd years after the writing of the play.

Perhaps we call it the Balcony Scene because on the Globe stage, there were two what-we-would-now-call balconies that were used for just this kind of moment. But more likely it's because of one of those arcane stories of theatre. As with all theatrical tales, it involves theft.

Nearly a hundred years after Shakespeare wrote R&J, the Balcony Scene was filched by the playwright Thomas Otway, who grafted the whole scene onto his play *The History and Fall of Caius Marius.* Substituting his own lovers' names ("Marius, Marius, wherefore art thou Marius?" — I kid you not), Otway explicitly places his young lady (Lavinia) on a balcony with Marius in the garden below.

(An aside — I would love to see a play about Caius Marius: his battle with Jugurtha, his war against the Germans, his role in the Italian War, his civil war against Sulla, his exile, and his mad return that turned Rome into an abattoir for thirteen days. Let us just say Otway's play ain't that play.)

Nevertheless, Otway's *Caius Marius* was a sensation, eclipsing Shakespeare's love story for a generation. When an enterprising theatre producer named David Garrick resurrected R&J in the early eighteenth century, he retained the part that everyone knew from Otway's play: the balcony.

It gets stranger. The actor who played Romeo in Garrick's production was a fellow called Spranger Barry. Barry left Garrick's theatre and staged his own version of R&J, stealing the same conceit. It is *this* production that was captured for all time in an etching, thus engraving the image of the balcony in the impressionable minds of producers and audiences forevermore. Truth is far stranger than fiction.

But in Shakespeare's text, there is no mention of a balcony. Instead, Romeo says window. "What light through yonder window breaks?"

This has always bothered me about this scene. It's not a balcony, it's a window. After years of snide remarks behind my hand, the last time I directed the show I finally did what I've long threatened: I got rid of Juliet's balcony entirely.

I'm sure I'm not the first. And I didn't do it to shock anybody. I wasn't trying to be postmodern, or to bite my thumb at convention — at least, not *just* to bite my thumb. I did it both to free the scene from the weight of expectation and literally free the actors to, you know, interact.

Here's what often happens. Romeo comes in and hides. Mercutio and the boys chase him, tease him, then leave. He comes out, sees her on the balcony, and hides again, close to the audience. But if he's going to see her, he either has to turn his back on the audience, or he has to be entirely across the stage — he's got lots of asides before he reveals himself. So there's always this physical gulf between them. And it lasts through the whole damned scene — *unless* you have him climb up to the balcony. But if he can do that, why does he need the cords two acts later?

So I decided to scrap the balcony and put the window Juliet's standing in on the ground floor.

It worked beautifully. What I liked best about it was Juliet's freedom, and the intimacy it allowed her to share with the audience. Juliet is a character forever put on a pedestal — by teachers, by readers, by actors, by directors, by audiences, all thinking her the ideal young lover. Placing her high on some balcony away from the audience reinforces that, whereas I always want to undermine it.

Why undermine? Because she's a thirteen year-old girl! She's not some savvy, romantic ideal. She's young, smart, funny, conflicted, bursting with too many emotions at once. She pingpongs from thought to thought, emotion to emotion, bubbling over with more than she can express, and not at all demure and sweet (see "The Juliet Trap").

(Note, too, that in my last production, Juliet wore pajamas. Not some flowing night-gown, but what an almost-fourteen-year-old wears to bed. Just like in the first Spider-Man movie, where Mary Jane is wearing pajamas, not a negligee. That's the way a young girl dresses!)

So, by removing the balcony, I freed both Juliet and the audience. It was great fun to allow Juliet to match her mental ricocheting with her physicality.

Now I'm the first to admit not every line is with me. Romeo has a reference to her "being o'er my head." But there are two or three other reasonable interpretations of that line. Likewise, I found ways to stage "One kiss and I'll descend" and "I see thee, now thou art so low, as one dead," both lines from the Morning-After scene, by using the window and a couple of steps. And the cords the Nurse brings? We used those to help Romeo get over the wall.

As I say, I'm sure I'm not the first to get rid of the balcony. But I went further with this idea than just putting Juliet on the ground floor. When Romeo ditches his friends, Benvolio says, "He ran this way, and leapt this orchard wall."

Romeo climbed a wall? Why not leave him up there?

Thus, for the first part of the scene, Romeo was up and Juliet down. He descended before the initial love talk was done, well before her "Farewell, compliment" speech. And suddenly it was a scene I had never seen before. We'd shaken off the baggage of preconceptions and could look at what these two people are actually saying.

What is the scene about, then, if not romance? It's about how wonderfully stupid teenagers in love are.

It, of course, begins with Romeo seeing Juliet in her balcony (window). He tells us all about the stuff we can see for ourselves; she's sighing, laying her hand upon her cheek — the same hand Romeo held and tried to kiss during the party.

By rights, this is the moment when he should step out and proclaim his love, swearing by the stars and God in Heaven how deeply he adores her, in return for which she might give him a glove, some token to carry to the end of his days as he pines for her. That's Courtly Love. It's pretty stupid, but those are the rules.

Instead, Romeo does something unthinkable in a Courtly Lover. He eavesdrops on her, listens to her most intimate thoughts — because they happen to be of him. She's repeating his name, just as Tony in *West Side Story* does with Maria. Then, in a moment of petulance, she asks why he has to be a Montague, pleading with him to renounce his family — or else she will.

> JULIET:
> *O Romeo, Romeo! wherefore art thou Romeo?*
> *Deny thy father and refuse thy name;*
> *Or, if thou wilt not, be but sworn my love,*
> *And I'll no longer be a Capulet.*

Romeo even asks the audience if he should talk, or go on listening:

> ROMEO:
> *[Aside] Shall I hear more, or shall I speak at this?*

JULIET:
'Tis but thy name that is my enemy;
Thou art thyself, though not a Montague.
What's Montague? it is nor hand, nor foot,
Nor arm, nor face, nor any other part
Belonging to a man. O, be some other name!
What's in a name? that which we call a rose
By any other name would smell as sweet;
So Romeo would, were he not Romeo call'd,
Retain that dear perfection which he owes
Without that title. Romeo, doff thy name,
And for that name which is no part of thee
Take all myself.

Thinking she's alone, she's very bold, even a little scandalous (it's adorable when Juliets blush even as they speak the line, "any other part belonging to a man").

Romeo listens until he can't contain himself any longer and leaps out of the bushes, shouting, "I take thee at thy word!"

At which she screams because there's a Peeping Tom in her garden.

Seriously, the scene can and should be as funny as it is sweet. There are plenty of moments for both. The genius of Shakespeare is his ability to so utterly inhabit each character he writes. And we all remember being those kids! We remember the awkwardness of love — does she love me, what must he think of me, did I sound stupid?

I have four favorite comedic moments in the scene. The first two come relatively early, back to back, as she's trying to compose herself after realizing he's overheard her give away the game. She starts talking and can't stop. Think of a thirteen-year-old girl going through the whole gamut of emotions — embarrassment, abandon, concern, trust, more concern, hope, even more concern, posturing, self-doubt, chastisement of him, and more self-doubt. Imagine, too, a boy trying to open his mouth at each piece of punctuation, unable to get a word in edgewise:

> JULIET:
> *Thou know'st the mask of night is on my face,*
> *Else would a maiden blush bepaint my cheek*
> *For that which thou hast heard me speak to-night*
> *Fain would I dwell on form, fain, fain deny*
> *What I have spoke: but farewell compliment!*
> *Dost thou love me? I know thou wilt say 'Ay,'*
> *And I will take thy word: yet if thou swear'st,*
> *Thou mayst prove false; at lovers' perjuries*
> *Then say, Jove laughs. O gentle Romeo,*
> *If thou dost love, pronounce it faithfully:*
> *Or if thou think'st I am too quickly won,*
> *I'll frown and be perverse an say thee nay,*
> *So thou wilt woo; but else, not for the world.*
> *In truth, fair Montague, I am too fond,*
> *And therefore thou mayst think my 'havior light:*
> *But trust me, gentleman, I'll prove more true*
> *Than those that have more cunning to be strange.*
> *I should have been more strange, I must confess,*
> *But that thou overheard'st, ere I was ware,*
> *My true love's passion: therefore pardon me,*
> *And not impute this yielding to light love,*
> *Which the dark night hath so discovered.*

And here's my next favorite bit of comedic timing. Belatedly, Romeo tries to play the lover, making grand oaths of love:

> ROMEO:
> *Lady, by yonder blessed moon I swear*
> *That tips with silver all these fruit-tree tops—*

JULIET:
O, swear not by the moon, the inconstant moon,
That monthly changes in her circled orb,
Lest that thy love prove likewise variable.

Romeo is confused. He knows a lover has to swear by something.

ROMEO:
What shall I swear by?

And Juliet says the sweetest thing:

JULIET:
Do not swear at all;
Or, if thou wilt, swear by thy gracious self,
Which is the god of my idolatry,
And I'll believe thee.

How beautiful is that? The only thing in the world that he could swear by is himself, because he is the only thing in the whole world that matters to her.

Being irredeemably stupid, Romeo starts to do it:

ROMEO:
If my heart's dear love–

JULIET:
Well, do not swear.

"Shhh. Don't talk, pretty boy. You'll spoil it.'"
That comic timing right there, coming right after the most wonderful sweetness —— that is some genius hilarity. It's like that wonderful line Mary Louise Parker had on her second

episode of *The West Wing*: "'Maybe not so much for you with the talking.'"

Next in the comedy goldmine comes a pair of lines that need no explanation:

ROMEO:
O, wilt thou leave me so unsatisfied?

JULIET:
What satisfaction canst thou have to-night?

But my favorite moment comes toward the end of the scene, where Romeo and Juliet are, in effect, two teens on the phone late at night:

JULIET:
I have forgot why I did call thee back.

ROMEO:
Let me stand here till thou remember it.

JULIET:
I shall forget, to have thee still stand there,
Remembering how I love thy company.

ROMEO:
And I'll still stay, to have thee still forget,
Forgetting any other home but this.

No, you hang up.
No, you hang up.
If played right, it is at least as funny as it is touching.
Just like the scene. Balcony or no.

The King and the Beggar

In the space between the party and the Window Scene, we have a terrific mockery of love performed by an inebriated Mercutio, with drunk Benvolio laughing and shushing him. Early on, Mercutio tries to summon Romeo by invoking "love":

MERCUTIO:
Romeo, Humours, Madman, Passion, Louer,
Appeare thou in the likenesse of a sigh,
Speake but one rime, and I am satisfied:
Cry me but ay me, Prouant, but Loue and day,
Speake to my goship Venus one faire word,
One Nickname for her purblind Sonne and her,
Young Abraham Cupid he that shot so true,
When King Cophetua lou'd the begger Maid,
He heareth not, he stirreth not, he mouethnot,
The Ape is dead, I must coniure him…

Of the many references he makes, one is clearly a favorite of Shakespeare's because he references it so often. No fewer than five times in four different plays, Shakespeare alludes to the story of King Cophetua (R&J, *Henry IV, Part 2; Much Ado About Nothing;* and, appropriately, twice in *Love's Labour's Lost.)* So too does Ben Johnson in *Every Man in His Humour*, which indicates the tale was popular enough to be well-known to Londoners. Some have advanced that there was a lost play about the lovestruck king, or else a poem or song. Alas, the first version we have of the tale is a poem published in 1612 by Richard Johnson in *A Crowne Garland of Goulden Roses*. With a nod to Ross W. Duffin's *Shakespeare's Songbook*, which is where I first discovered it, I offer the whole poem here:

> *I read that once in Affrica*
> *A princely right did raine,*
> *Who had to name Cophetua,*
> *As poets they did faine:*
> *From natures lawes he did decline,*
> *For sure he was not of my mind.*
> *He cared not for women-kinde,*
> *But did them all disdaine.*
> *But marke what hapened on a day,*
> *As he out of his window lay,*
> *He saw a beggar all in gray,*
> *The which did cause his paine.*
>
> *The blinded boy, that shootes so trim,*
> *From heaven downe did hie;*
> *He drew a dart and shot at him,*
> *In place where he did lye:*
> *Which soone did pierse him to the quicke,*
> *And when he felt the arrow pricke,*
> *Which in his tender heart did sticke,*
> *He looketh as he would dye.*
> *"What sudden chance is this," quoth he,*
> *"That I to love must subject be,*
> *Which never thereto would agree,*
> *But still did it defie?"*

Then from the window he did come,
And laid him on his bed,
A thousand heapes of care did runne
Within his troubled head:
For now he meanes to crave her love,
And now he seekes which way to prove
How he his fancie might remoove,
And not this beggar wed.
But Cupid had him so in snare,
That this poor begger must prepare
A salve to cure him of his care,
Or els he would be dead.

And, as he musing thus did lye,
He thought for to devise
How he might have her companye,
That so did 'maze his eyes.
"In thee," quoth he, "doth rest my life;
For surely thou shalt be my wife,
Or else this hand with bloody knife
The Gods shall sure suffice."
Then from his bed he soon arose,
And to his pallace gate he goes;
Full little then this begger knowes
When she the king espies.

"The Gods preserve your majesty,"
The beggers all 'gain cry:
"Vouchsafe to give your charity
Our childrens food to buy."
The king to them his purse did cast,
And they to part it made great haste;
This silly woman was the last
That after them did hye.
The king he cal'd her back againe,

And unto her he gave his chaine;
And said, "With us you shal remaine
Till such time as we dye.

"For thou," quoth he, "shalt be my wife,
And honoured for my queene;
With thee I meane to lead my life,
As shortly shall be seene:
Our wedding shall appointed be,
And every thing in its degree:
Come on," quoth he, "and follow me,
Thou shalt go shift thee cleane.
What is thy name, faire maid?" quoth he.
"Penelophon, O king," quoth she;
With that she made a lowe courtsey;
A trim one as I weene.

Thus hand in hand along they walke
Unto the king's pallace:
The king with curteous comly talke
This beggar doth imbrace:
The begger blusheth scarlet red,
And straight againe as pale as lead,
But not a word at all she said,
She was in such amaze.
At last she spake with trembling voyce,
And said, "O king, I doe rejoyce
That you wil take me from your choyce,
And my degree's so base."

And when the wedding day was come,
The king commanded strait
The noblemen both all and some
Upon the queene to wait.
And she behaved herself that day,

As if she had never walkt the way;
She had forgot her gown of gray,
Which she did weare of late.
The proverbe old is come to passe,
The priest, when he begins his masse,
Forgets that ever clerke he was;
He knowth not his estate.

Here you may read, Cophetua,
Though long time fancie-fed,
Compelled by the blinded boy
The begger for to wed:
He that did lovers lookes disdaine,
To do the same was glad and faine,
Or else he would himselfe have slaine,
In storie, as we read.
Disdaine no whit, O lady deere,
But pitty now thy servant heere,
Least that it hap to thee this yeare,
As to that king it did.

And thus they led a quiet life
Duringe their princely raigne;
And in a tombe were buried both,
As writers sheweth plaine.
The lords they tooke it grievously,
The ladies tooke it heavily,
The commons cryed pitiously,
Their death to them was paine,
Their fame did sound so passingly,
That it did pierce the starry sky,
And throughout all the world did flye
To every prince's realme.

Some feel the last two stanzas should exchange places, and I agree.

One can see how the tale of a man who swears never to love being felled by Cupid's arrow would have an appeal to so many of Shakespeare's characters. Benedick jokes about it - 'hang me up at the door of a brothel-house for the sign of blind Cupid' - and Don Adriano says to Mote, 'Is there not a ballad, boy of the blind king and the beggar?' Most apt is Mercutio, however, comparing Romeo to the king. Later he will say of Romeo:

MERUCTIO:
Alas poore Romeo, he is already dead, stab'd with a white wenches blacke eye, runne through the eare with Love song, the very pinne of his heart cleft with the blind Bowe-boyes but-shaft.

To Mercutio, being struck with love is as good as being dead. Or at least, the Romeo they knew has been killed. Benedick shares the same sentiment about Claudio:

BENEDICK:
Is't come to this? In faith, hath not the world one man but he will wear his cap with suspicion? Shall I never see a bachelor of threescore again? Go to, i' faith, an thou wiltneeds thrust thy neck into a yoke, wear the print of it, and sigh away Sundays.'

Yet for all their protestations, it's a tale that continued to resonate for at least two more centuries. There's Edmund Blair Leighton's painting *The King and the Beggar-Maid,* and a truly gorgeous painting entitled *King Cophetua and the Beggar Maid* by Sir Edward Coley Burne-Jones hanging in the Tate Gallery in London, inspired by a short poem Tennyson wrote in 1833:

Her arms across her breast she laid;
She was more fair than words can say:
Bare-footed came the beggar maid
Before the king Cophetua.
In robe and crown the king stept down,
To meet and greet her on her way;
"It is no wonder," said the lords,
"She is more beautiful than day."

As shines the moon in clouded skies,
She in her poor attire was seen:
One praised her ancles, one her eyes,
One her dark hair and lovesome mien:
So sweet a face, such angel grace,
In all that land had never been:
Cophetua sware a royal oath:
"This beggar maid shall be my queen!"

In fact, Lewis Carroll's most famous photograph, in a collection at the Metropolitan Museum of Art in New York, is of young Alice Liddell in 1858 in the role of the "beggar girl" from this story.

It's only in the last century that this story has ceased to resonate — or rather, been replaced with a whole new set of references. The film *Pretty Woman* comes to mind.

Ratcatcher

Speaking of Mercutio's songifying…

Thrice Mercutio refers to Tybalt as a cat, once behind his back as "more than the Prince of Cats" and twice to his face as both "Rat-catcher" and "King of Cats."

This is most likely a reference to his name, which is very like the French Thibauld, and therefore resonant of Tibert the Cat in the "Reynard the Fox" fables, thus casting Mercutio into the role of the fox who keeps tricking the cat and therefore costing him his lives.

There is another tradition, however, of a folk tale that was popular in the 1550s of the "King of Cats." In 1563 the poet William Baldwin published a version of this story which is both the first long-form horror story in English and also reputed to be the first English novel. It has to do with a creature like a werewolf and a whole underworld society of cats.

In some versions of the tale, a traveler hears a talking cat relating to him there is to be a funeral of a person with a similar name. The traveler reaches his destination and tells the story, whereupon a house cat cries, "Then I am the King of Cats" and races up a chimney.

He may also be referencing the song "The Ratcatcher":

There was a rare Rat-catcher,
did about the country wander,
The soundest blade of all his trade,
or I should him deeply slander:
For still would he cry, a Rat a tat,
tarra rat, ever:
To catch a mouse, or to carouse,
such a Ratter I saw never.

There are 24 verses, so I will spare you, though you can find them all in *Shakespeare's Songbook*.

Mercutio seems often to break into song, if only to reference popular music. All we know of "An Old Hare Whore" is that it is a song, and that only because the Bad Quarto mentions he sings it.

But all of the cat references are to Tybalt. Hell, after Mercutio is stabbed, he cries, "What, a Dog, a Rat, a Mouse, a Cat to scratch a man to death!" It speaks to his opinion of Tybalt, which is that he is a poseur, an annoyance. We can infer from Mab that Mercutio has seen something of the world. His contempt for Tybalt comes from the Capulet's exact lack of experience. Just after that line, he condemns Tybalt as "a Braggart, a Rogue, a Villaine, that fights by the booke of Arithmeticke."

Earlier, when he hears that Tybalt has sent a challenge to Romeo's house, he momentarily seems to have respect for Tybalt's skill, before eviscerating him on the altar of his wit.

MERCUTIO:
And is he a man to encounter Tybalt?

BENVOLIO:
Why what is Tibalt?

MERCUTIO:

More then Prince of Cats. Oh hee's the Couragious Captaine of Complements: he fights as you sing pricksong, keeps time, distance, and proportion, he rests his minum, one, two, and the third in your bosom: the very butcher of a silk button, a Dualist, a Dualist: a Gentleman of the very first house of the first and second cause: ah the immortall Passado, the Punto reuerso, the Hay.

BENVOLIO:
The what?

MERCUTIO:
The Pox of such antique lisping affecting phantacies, these new tuners of accent: Iesu a very good blade, a very tall man, a very good whore. Why is not this a lamentable thing Grandsire, that we should be thus afflicted with these strange flies: these fashion Mongers, these pardon-mee's, who stand so much on the new form, that they cannot sit at ease on the old bench. O their bones, their bones.

You can feel the disdain for the new breed of man, these "duelists," who put on airs and learn to fight out of books, taught their "fence" by dancing masters instead. As in *As You Like It*, where Touchstone elaborates on the "seventh cause" of courtiers' dueling, showing the absurdity of Retort Courteous and the Quip Modest, Mercutio has no respect for such men as Tybalt. Perhaps that's why he's so outraged at Romeo's submission to Tybalt, causing him to draw his own sword. "O calme, dishonourable, vile submission! Alla stucatho carries it away."

"Alla stocatta" is an Italian term for the thrust, but being spoken in Italian and used as a term for Tybalt, it becomes one more example of Mercutio's disdain for Capulet's nephew — a disdain that, with a little help from Romeo, costs him his life.

The Art of Mis-timing Part I

One of the hats I wear is Fight Director, choreographing violence for the stage.

While it's easy to get caught up in the fun of swashbuckling, the real challenge is to make violence on stage seem as awful as it is in life. It's gotten harder in the last few decades, as we as a society have become more and more inured to images of violence.

So I'm going to share the secret of great stage violence with you. Lean closer.

It's about *story*.

A good fight is not about cool moves. It's not about blood or violence. A fight is like any conflict — it's a tale of desire and denial.

> *Desire: I want your life.*
> *Denial: You can't have it.*

It's almost romantic, and combatants have just as much intimacy as lovers. Sex and violence — two sides of the same coin. Both are all about desire.

This is something fight directors understand. They also understand pushing boundaries — not with blood, but with story.

So let's spend a few moments discussing the fights in R&J.

I don't take the opening brawl in R&J particularly seriously. If you give Italian men swords on a hot summer's day and send them out into the street where there are women to impress, what are they going to do? They're going to fight.

Also, we know that this is the third such brawl in recent days. If someone had been killed, the Prince would be taking this much more seriously. He wouldn't be threatening a fine, or impotently saying he'll execute the next person who starts a fight. He'd do something.

So the opening brawl becomes about one-upmanship, about showing off, about teens being teens.

The same could be said about the Mercutio-Tybalt fight, to a much more heightened degree. Tybalt isn't trying to kill Mercutio.

Let me repeat that — *Tybalt is not trying to kill Mercutio.*

Why not? Because he'd be a dead man. Kill the Prince's cousin? Tybalt's a hothead, but he's not stupid. In fact, at the start of the scene, he does everything he can to avoid Mercutio's challenges. It's only when Mercutio goads him with jabs to his past endurance that he draws and they fight.

When I stage this, it's always about showing off. There's danger, sure, but there's also laughter. They're not going for the kill; they're going for the humiliation. "Come, sir, your passado." That's a taunt, not a vow of murderous intent. Mercutio's disdain for Tybalt doesn't include murder. It is just about showing up the fancy boy.

The only reason the fight turns deadly is that it's interrupted. Romeo darts into the mix, thrusting himself between the combatants, thinking to stop the fight. In that split second, an "envious thrust from Tybalt took the life of stout Mercutio."

Mercutio himself says as much. "Why the devil came you between us? I was hurt under your arm." It wasn't supposed to happen this way — and would not have, but for Romeo trying to stop the fight.

That's the art of mis-timing. They say Comedy is all about timing. So to turn a Comedy into a Tragedy, all one requires is an exquisite moment of mis-timing. As happens here.

I love the laughter that turns to silence in this scene. If we can get the audience laughing at the fight, and especially at Mercutio as he's dying, then they are ripe for the reveal that he's actually dead. Done well, it sucks the air right from their lungs. Making Mercutio die before their eyes without their knowing it makes them complicit in his death, and allows them to share in Romeo's guilt and despair.

Mercutio dies, and Tybalt runs off, only to return. I usually tell my Tybalts they're coming back to see if Mercutio is okay — again, if he's killed the Prince's cousin, he's in huge trouble.

Hearing that Mercutio is indeed dead, Tybalt blames the true cause of that death: Romeo.

Romeo, too, knows he's to blame. But so is Tybalt. Picking up Mercutio's sword, he declares:

> *Mercutios soule*
> *Is but a little way above our heads,*
> *Staying for thine to keepe him companie:*
> *Either thou or I, or both, must goe with him.*

In contrast to the earlier display of swordsmanship, this is the vicious fight, the nasty, brutal, terrifying, no-holds-barred fight. This fight is about swords and daggers and knees and teeth and fists. This is a fight to the death.

One tradition that I've always disliked is Romeo's "accidental" win. You see it best in the Zeffirelli film, where a beaten Romeo is on the ground, sprawled. Tybalt races at him to finish him off, Romeo sticks out his sword in blind desperation, and Tybalt impales himself on the end of Romeo's sword. Really? It's a story, but not one I like.

I tend to have my Romeo win in a nasty way — a dagger to the belly, a sword across the neck. Whatever it is, he's pumped, he's angry, he's victorious. *"Fire-eyed fury"* is indeed his conduct now. It's only when he looks at Tybalt lying dead at his feet that he even starts to think again. And the progression of his thoughts goes like this:

> *I did it.*
> *I killed him.*
> *I killed the man who killed Mercutio.*
> *I killed the man who killed my best friend.*
> *I killed Tybalt.*
> *I killed… my wife's cousin.*
> *Juliet's cousin!*
>
> 'O, I am Fortune's Fool!'

Now *that's* a story.

The Quartet

Immediately after the deaths of Mercutio and Tybalt, seconds after the Prince banishes Romeo from Verona, we get one of the best and brightest speeches in the play — Juliet eagerly anticipating her wedding night.

I love the speech, and I love the scene. There's only one problem. It goes on way too long.

The same can be said for the scene that follows it, where the Friar argues with Romeo about their present luckless state. Great character stuff, wonderful lines. But just waaaay too long, man.

This is not a problem with Shakespeare. It's a problem with me and with modern audiences in general. We're used to a three-act structure, where the climax comes at the end. Shakespeare wrote in a five-act structure, where the climax comes right in the middle, and the last two acts are watching the consequences play out. By the end of the Friar's scene with Romeo, there's a new plan in place, and the story picks up momentum again. But until then, it's all angst—wonderful angst, amazing angst—to no purpose. I don't care how good your Juliet is, or your Romeo. We've just come off a pair of sword fights, and we're in an emotional stupor. We need the next two scenes to move us through it and back into the story.

Having read my earlier pieces, you're probably expecting me to say, "Cut 'em!" No. They're too good. You can't cut them — not Act III Scene ii, nor Act III Scene iii. There's way too much good stuff in there to lose.

But you can combine them.

The two scenes are written as mirrors, complementing each other. An agonized teen railing against fate, a wiser adult counseling them (though I don't know how wise the Nurse is).

I saw this done once at Chicago Shakespeare Theatre, in a production directed by Kim Rubinstein, and I thought it was brilliant. I'd done similar intercutting when I directed *Richard III*, merging the two speeches to the armies at the end. (Like my director friend Kevin Theis says, "Get on with it! We can smell the ending!" Here we're not at the ending, but the show invariably lags.) By taking the mirrored scenes and merging them into one, we preserve all the great lines, and yet have real momentum.

My sole regret is that we lose the Nurse arriving in Friar Lawrence's cell, allowing Romeo's plaintive, "O Nurse!" But outside of that, I love this cutting with a passion.

So here it is, in Folio format, which is how we roll in our house. Imagine, as you read, the two scenes happening simultaneously, on the same stage.

Enjoy!

(Enter Juliet alone)

JULIET:
Gallop apace, you fiery footed steedes,
And bring in Cloudie night immediately.
Spred thy close Curtaine Love-performing night,
That run-awayes eyes may wincke, and Romeo
Leape to these armes, untalkt of and unseene,
Come night, come Romeo, come thou day in night,
For thou wilt lie upon the wings of night

Whiter then new Snow upon a Ravens backe:
Come gentle night, come loving blackebrow'd night.
Give me my Romeo, and when I shall die,
Take him and cut him out in little starres,
And he will make the Face of heaven so fine,
That all the world will be in Love with night,
And pay no worship to the Garish Sun.
O I have bought the Mansion of a Love,
But not possest it, and though I am sold,
Not yet enjoy'd. O here comes my Nurse:

(Enter NURSE with cords)

JULIET:
And she brings newes and every tongue that speaks
But Romeos, name, speakes heavenly eloquence:
Now Nurse, what newes? what hast thou there?
The Cords that Romeo bid thee fetch?

NURSE:
I, I, the Cords.

JULIET:
Ay me, what newes?
Why dost thou wring thy hands.

NURSE:
A weladay, hee's dead, hee's dead,
We are undone Lady, we are undone.
Alacke the day, hee's gone, hee's kil'd, he's dead.

JULIET:
Can heaven be so envious?

NURSE:
Romeo can,
Though heaven cannot. O Romeo, Romeo.
Who ever would have thought it Romeo.

JULIET:
What divell art thou,
That dost torment me thus?
This torture should be roar'd in dismall hell,
Hath Romeo slaine himselfe?

NURSE:
I saw the wound, I saw it with mine eyes,
God saue the marke, here on his manly brest,
A pitteous Coarse, a bloody piteous Coarse:
Pale, pale as ashes, all bedawb'd in blood,
All in gore blood, I sounded at the sight-

JULIET:
O breake my heart,
Poore Banckrout breake at once,
To prison eyes, nere looke on libertie.
Vile earth to earth resigne, end motion here,
And thou and Romeo presse on heavie beere.

(Enter Friar Lawrence)

FRIAR:
Romeo come forth,
Come forth thou fearfull man,
Affliction is enamor'd of thy parts:
And thou art wedded to calamitie.

ROMEO:
Father what newes?

What is the Princes Doome?
What sorrow craves acquaintance at my hand,
That I yet know not?

FRIAR:
A gentler judgement vanisht from his lips,
Not bodies death, but bodies banishment.

ROMEO:
Ha, banishment? be mercifull, say death:
For exile hath more terror in his looke,
Much more then death: do not say banishment.

NURSE:
O curteous Tybalt honest Gentleman,
That ever I should live to see thee dead.

JULIET:
Is Romeo slaughtred? and is Tybalt dead?
My dearest Cozen, and my dearer Lord:

NURSE:
Tybalt is gone, and Romeo banished,
Romeo that kil'd him, he is banished.

FRIAR:
Here from Verona art thou banished:
Be patient, for the world is broad and wide.

ROMEO:
There is no world without Verona walles,
But Purgatorie, Torture, hell it selfe:
Hence banished: is banisht from the world.

JULIET:
O God! Did Rome'os hand shed Tybalts blood

NURSE:
It did, it did, alas the day, it did.

FRIAR:
O deadly sin, O rude unthankefulnesse!
Thy falt our Law calles death, but the kind Prince
Taking thy part, hath rusht aside the Law,
And turn'd that blacke word death, to banishment.
This is deare mercy, and thou seest it not.

JULIET:
Did ever Dragon keepe so faire a Cave?
Beautifull Tyrant, fiend Angelicall:
O Nature! what had'st thou to doe in hell,
When thou did'st bower the spirit of a fiend
In mortall paradise of such sweet flesh?

ROMEO:
'Tis Torture and not mercy, heaven is here
Where Juliet lives, and every Cat and Dog,
And little Mouse, every unworthy thing
Live here in Heaven and may looke on her,
But Romeo may not. hee is banished.
Had'st thou no poyson mixt, no sharpe ground knife,
No sudden meane of death, though nere so meane,
But banished to kill me? Banished?
O Frier, the damned use that word in hell:

NURSE:
There's no trust, no faith, no honestie in men,
All periur'd, all forsworne, all naught, all dissemblers,
Shame come to Romeo.

JULIET:
Blister'd be thy tongue

For such a wish, he was not borne to shame:
Upon his brow shame is asham'd to sit.
O what a beast was I to chide him?

NURSE:
Will you speake well of him,
That kil'd your Cozen?

JULIET:
Shall I speake ill of him that is my husband?
Ah poore my Lord, what tongue shall smooth thy name,
When I thy three houres wife have mangled it.
But wherefore Villaine did'st thou kill my Cozin?

FRIAR:
Then fond Mad man, heare me speake.

ROMEO:
O thou wilt speake againe of banishment.

JULIET:
My husband lives that Tibalt would have slaine,
And Tibalt dead that would have slaine my husband:
All this is comfort, wherefore weepe I then?

FRIAR:
Ile give thee Armour to keepe off that word,
Adversities sweete milke, Philosophie,
To comfort thee, though thou art banished.

JULIET:
Tybalt is dead and Romeo banished.

ROMEO:
Yet banished?

JULIET:
That banished, that one word banished,
Hath slaine ten thousand Tibalts.

ROMEO:
Hang up Philosophie:
Unlesse Philosophie can make a Juliet,
Displant a Towne, reverse a Princes Doome,
It helpes not, it prevailes not, talke no more.

FRIAR:
O then I see, that Mad men have no eares.

ROMEO:
How should they,
When wisemen have no eyes?

JULIET:
Romeo is banished to speake that word,
Is Father, Mother, Tybalt, Romeo, Juliet,
All slaine, all dead: Romeo is banished,
There is no end, no limit, measure, bound,
In that words death, no words can that woe sound.

FRIAR:
Let me dispute with thee of thy estate.

ROMEO:
Thou can'st not speake of that y dost not feele,
Wert thou as young as I, Juliet thy Love:
An houre but married, Tybalt murdered,
Doting like me, and like me banished,
Then mightest thou speake,
Then mightest thou teare thy hayre,
And fall upon the ground as I doe now,

Taking the measure of an vnmade grave.

JULIET:
Take up those Cordes, poore ropes you are beguil'd,
Both you and I for Romeo is exild:
He made you for a high-way to my bed,
But I a Maid, die Maiden widowed.

ROMEO:
Oh tell me Frier, tell me,
In what vile part of this Anatomie
Doth my name lodge?

JULIET:
Come Cords, come Nurse, Ile to my wedding bed,
And death not Romeo, take my Maiden head.

ROMEO:
Tell me, that I may sacke
The hatefull Mansion.

NURSE:
No—

FRIAR:
Hold thy desperate hand:
Art thou a man? thy forme cries out thou art:
Thy teares are womanish, thy wild acts denote
The unreasonable Furie of a beast.
Hast thou slaine Tybalt? wilt thou slay thy selfe?
And slay thy Lady, that in thy life lies,
By doing damned hate upon thy selfe?
What, rowse thee man, thy Juliet is alive,
There art thou happy. Tybalt would kill thee,
But thou slew'st Tybalt, there art thou happie.

The law that threatned death became thy Friend,
And turn'd it to exile, there art thou happy.
A packe or blessing light upon thy backe,
Happinesse Courts thee in her best array,
Goe get thee to thy Love as was decreed,
Ascend her Chamber, hence and comfort her.

NURSE:
Hie to your Chamber, Ile find Romeo
To comfort you, I wot well where he is:
Harke ye your Romeo will be heere at night.

FRIAR:
But looke thou stay not till the watch be set,
For then thou canst not passe to Mantua,
Where thou shalt live till we can finde a time
To blaze your marriage, reconcile your Friends,
Beg pardon of thy Prince, and call thee backe,
With twenty hundred thousand times more joy
Then thou went'st forth in lamentation.

(Exeunt)

Family Dysfunction

Theatre people create a shorthand for referring to scenes. Some are obvious: the Opening Brawl, Juliet's House, Mab, the Party, the Balcony Scene (yes, we all use it), Grey-Eyed Morn, the Wedding, the Fight, the Apothecary, the Tomb, etc. Some are tongue-in-cheek, such as the Morning After scene, when Romeo sneaks out after his one night with Juliet. Some just derive from the character who appears (Friar John) or a weird little line (Dates and Quinces).

Some are specific to the production, like the Quartet. And some have a shorthand so long in use that I have no idea from whence they originated. When Juliet is found "dead" after drinking the Friar's potion, that is traditionally called the Weeping and Wailing scene. Accurate, but not explicitly so named.

For as long as I can remember, the scene where Juliet enrages her father by refusing to marry Paris has been called the Family Dysfunction scene. It immediately follows the Morning After, which means Juliet is already distraught when her mother enters.

It's worth pausing a moment to appreciate Lady Capulet. The only mother of any of Shakespeare's Italian women to survive, she's certainly not a passive character. She's the one pushing the Paris marriage, which I find fascinating, especially in light of what we learn about her.

Telling Juliet that nearly fourteen is a little old to be getting married, she says, "I was your Mother, much upon these yeares that you are now a Maide." I often see this played as Lady Cap lying about her age. But Shakespeare's characters don't generally lie, and when they do, they tell us so.

Even more telling is Capulet's line in the previous scene with Paris:

PARIS:
Younger than she, are happy mothers made.

CAPULET:
And too soone mar'd are those so early made.

Often played with Lady Cap standing right there, even if the line is not meant as a direct insult, it connects to the following line about Capulet having lost other children ("Earth hath swallowed all my hopes but she"). How did they die? In childbirth? As infants? We know, at least, that Juliet had older siblings.

So Lady Cap was a mother by the time she was thirteen, which means marriage at twelve—to a man at least five years older, perhaps as much as twenty. She has lost all her children save Juliet, who she allows to basically be raised by the Nurse.

So when she arrives with the news that the young, handsome, noble, rich Paris wants to marry Juliet, she simply cannot understand her daughter's reluctance. "Verona's Summer hath not such a flower." Like a good parent, she is giving her daughter everything she never had, and cannot fathom why Juliet doesn't appreciate it.

Even more revealing about her character is her reaction to Tybalt's death. Her language is so passionate and vitriolic as to be shocking:

LADY CAPULET:
He is a kinsman to the Montague,
Affection makes him false, he speakes not true:
Some twenty of them fought in this blacke strife,
And all those twenty could but kill one life.
I beg for Justice, which thou Prince must give:
Romeo slew Tybalt, Romeo must not live.

Note that Capulet himself is none too sad to see Tybalt dead. While Lady Cap screams her head off, he says not a word. Not a single word. In fact, his comments about Tybalt are shockingly casual. Talking of Juliet's tears:

CAPULET:
Looke you, she Lou'd her kinsman Tybalt dearely,
And so did I. Well, we were borne to die.

Really? "We were born to die"? That's all he's moved to say? Clearly he is not broken up over Tybalt's untimely death.

Whereas Lady Cap is planning to murder Romeo herself. We learn this just after Romeo has crept out Juliet's window:

LADY CAPULET:
We will haue vengeance for it, feare thou not.
Then weepe no more, Ile send to one in Mantua,
Where that same banisht Run-agate doth liue,
Shall giue him such an vnaccustom'd dram,
That he shall soone keepe Tybalt company:
And then I hope thou wilt be satisfied.

Holy St. Francis! And that's just the beginning to the surprises in this scene. Informed she is betrothed to Paris, Juliet refuses, to her mother's disgust. Lord Cap comes in, ever the doting father, and comforts her — until he learns she won't wed the man he's chosen for her. Then he becomes a tyrant, a towering inferno of paternal rage.

> CAPULET
> *Hang thee young baggage, disobedient wretch,*
> *I tell thee what, get thee to Church a Thursday,*
> *Or never after looke me in the face.*
> *Speake not, reply not, do not answere me.*
> *My fingers itch!*

He's on the verge of hitting her! Capulet, who adores his daughter, has turned on a dime and is now threatening her unless she marries the man he's chosen. He threatens the Nurse and rages about how he's spent all his waking hours making a good match for this "disobedient wretch," who he advices to marry Paris, or else "hang, beg, starve, die in the streets!"

In desperation, Juliet turns to her mother, who washes her hands:

> LADY CAPULET:
> *Talke not to me, for Ile not speake a word,*
> *Do as thou wilt, for I haue done with thee.*

Even Juliet's beloved Nurse, who knows the truth, betrays her, telling her to marry Paris.

Leaving Juliet entirely alone.

Family Dysfunction is the name of the scene where Juliet's family finally reveal themselves for who they are.

Tybalt's Ghost

It amazes me that, of the twenty-odd productions I've been a part of and the dozen more I've seen, I'm the only director to make use of these lines:

> JULIET:
> *O, look! methinks I see my cousin's ghost*
> *Seeking out Romeo, that did spit his body*
> *Upon a rapier's point: stay, Tybalt, stay!*
> *Romeo, I come! this do I drink to thee.*

She says she sees the ghost! I cannot fathom why directors ignore this. She straight-up says that she sees the ghost!

It seems a wonderful (and obvious) device to have dead Tybalt enter, covered "all in blood, all in gore blood," as the Nurse describes him, and search for Romeo. It is also great motivation for Juliet to drink the Friar's potion, which until that moment she has been talking herself out of doing. I've used this twice, and it's frightfully creepy.

Yet I've only ever seen the ghost in my own productions. So perhaps I am simply insane. But I think this is one of the most powerful points in the show. The creators of *West Side Story* surely thought so — they staged an entire dream ballet around it.

She's Not Dead Yet!

Ask anyone who has ever played Lord or Lady Capulet, and especially any Nurse, to name their least favorite scene, and they'll tell you it's the Weeping and Wailing scene.

The Weeping and Wailing scene is where Juliet's drunk the potion and everyone loses their minds. I've long had a pet peeve about this scene, but it was my wife who really figured it out. Both of us come at it from the same place, and it's the same thing that drives us both crazy. Most directors miss this. They forget one simple, true fact:

She's not dead yet.

At the moment that her family discovers her, Juliet is in fact alive and well. Everything is going according to plan. Again, it's the same plan from *Much Ado* — we'll pretend she's dead and everything will be all right.

So the family's grief seems utterly out of place. The Friar knows she's not dead. The audience knows she's not dead. So why do we have to go through the motions of grief?

It was Jan who noted how badly written the grief in this scene is. Don't get me wrong, Shakespeare can write grief:

HORATIO:
Now cracks a noble heart. Good night sweet prince:
And flights of angels sing thee to thy rest!

Or even later in R&J, Lady Capulet says:

LADY CAPULET:
O me! this sight of death is as a bell,
That warns my old age to a sepulchre.

Shakespeare's grief is often like this — brief. As if the speaker lacks the words. Whereas the grief in the Weeping and Wailing scene is anything but brief:

FRIAR LAURENCE:
Come, is the bride ready to go to church?

CAPULET:
Ready to go, but never to return.
O son! the night before thy wedding-day
Hath Death lain with thy wife. There she lies,
Flower as she was, deflowered by him.
Death is my son-in-law, Death is my heir;
My daughter he hath wedded: I will die,
And leave him all; life, living, all is Death's.

PARIS:
Have I thought long to see this morning's face,
And doth it give me such a sight as this?

LADY CAPULET:
Accursed, unhappy, wretched, hateful day!
Most miserable hour that e'er time saw
In lasting labour of his pilgrimage!
But one, poor one, one poor and loving child,
But one thing to rejoice and solace in,
And cruel death hath catch'd it from my sight!

NURSE:
O woe! O woful, woful, woful day!
Most lamentable day, most woful day,
That ever, ever, I did yet behold!
O day! O day! O day! O hateful day!
Never was seen so black a day as this:
O woful day, O woful day!

PARIS:
Beguiled, divorced, wronged, spited, slain!
Most detestable death, by thee beguil'd,
By cruel cruel thee quite overthrown!
O love! O life! not life, but love in death!

CAPULET:
Despised, distressed, hated, martyr'd, kill'd!
Uncomfortable Time, why camest thou now
To murder, murder our solemnity?
O child! O child! my soul, and not my child!
Dead art thou! Alack! my child is dead;
And with my child my joys are buried.

Look at those exclamation points. Look at those ecphonetic Os. This is not subtle grief. These are not heartbreaking words that rend the soul of the hearer.

No, this is Italian opera.

Take those speeches and overlap them, let the characters embrace their Italianness, and suddenly the audience is laughing. As they should be! Because at the moment, *everything is working*.

This was my wife's idea, playing off of my love for the end of the scene. Because it's the end that convinces me the whole thing is supposed to be funny, as Paris entered the scene with a set of musicians.

Second aside — I feel really bad for Paris. He'd be the hero of any other play. He's a good guy, and his story arc is just awful — fall for girl, ask girl's dad to marry her, dance with girl, get permission from dad, see girl at church, go to marry her and find her dead, take flowers to her tomb and get killed. There is nothing wrong with Paris. Just like everybody else, he's simply star-cross'd.

Back to the end of the scene. Everybody leaves, except for the Nurse, the servant Peter, and the musicians, who have the following exchange:

FIRST MUSICIAN:
Faith, we may put up our pipes, and be gone.

NURSE:
Honest goodfellows, ah, put up, put up;
For, well you know, this is a pitiful case. (Exit)

FIRST MUSICIAN:
Ay, by my troth, the case may be amended.

(Enter PETER)

PETER:
Musicians, O, musicians, 'Heart's ease, Heart's
ease:' O, an you will have me live, play 'Heart's ease.'

FIRST MUSICIAN:
Why 'Heart's ease?'

PETER:
O, musicians, because my heart itself plays 'My
heart is full of woe:' O, play me some merry dump,
to comfort me.

FIRST MUSICIAN:
Not a dump we; 'tis no time to play now.

PETER:
You will not, then?

FIRST MUSICIAN:
No.

PETER:
I will then give it you soundly.

FIRST MUSICIAN:
What will you give us?

PETER:
No money, on my faith, but the gleek;
I will give you the minstrel.

FIRST MUSICIAN:
Then I will give you the serving-creature.

PETER:
Then will I lay the serving-creature's dagger on your pate. I will carry no crotchets: I'll re you, I'll fa you; do you note me?

FIRST MUSICIAN:
An you re us and fa us, you note us.

SECOND MUSICIAN:
Pray you, put up your dagger, and put out your wit.

PETER:
Then have at you with my wit! I will dry-beat you with an iron wit, and put up my iron dagger. Answer

me like men:
'When griping grief the heart doth wound,
And doleful dumps the mind oppress,
Then music with her silver sound'–
why 'silver sound'? why 'music with her silver
sound'? What say you, Simon Catling?

FIRST MUSICIAN:
Marry, sir, because silver hath a sweet sound.

PETER:
Pretty! What say you, Hugh Rebeck?

SECOND MUSICIAN:
I say 'silver sound,' because musicians sound for silver.

PETER:
Pretty too! What say you, James Soundpost?

THIRD MUSICIAN:
Faith, I know not what to say.

PETER:
O, I cry you mercy; you are the singer: I will say
for you. It is 'music with her silver sound,'
because musicians have no gold for sounding:
'Then music with her silver sound
With speedy help doth lend redress.' (Exit)

FIRST MUSICIAN:
What a pestilent knave is this same!

SECOND MUSICIAN:
Hang him, Jack! Come, we'll in here; tarry for the
mourners, and stay dinner.

Okay, it's not Shakespeare at his best (it's funny because no musician ever passes up free food — get it?).

Still, it's clearly comedy. Shakespeare wanted us laughing at the end of this scene. And I tend to trust his instincts.

The Art of Mis-timing Part II

Back to violence, and mis-timing.

Skipping the death of Paris, which I always make quick, ("We can smell the ending!"), we come to the double suicide.

Romeo first. He drinks the poison, then he has these lines:

ROMEO:
O true apothecary!
Thy drugs are quick. Thus with a kiss I die.

Now, it all hangs on where you place the kiss. There's a perfectly good place for it earlier:

ROMEO:
Arms, take your last embrace! and, lips, O you
The doors of breath, seal with a righteous kiss
A dateless bargain to engrossing death!

But nobody makes that the last kiss. Besides, those lines are usually cut — they sound too much like Pyramus.

So does Romeo kiss her before "Thus with a kiss I die" or after?

Usually, I see it before. Drink potion, kiss girl, say last line, drop dead.

I like to put it after. Here's the progression: drink potion, say last line, lean down to kiss her—

And she moves.

Romeo stops, stunned. Imagine the flood of emotion following that moment. The joy, followed by the horror.

Oh god. She's alive! Juliet's alive!

Oh god, I just drank poison...

Romeo struggles to fight the poison he just drank, trying to make himself vomit, working in vain to stop the death that's closing in on him now, even as he's watching her wake up. He falls, reaching for her. Maybe he even hears the Friar's voice as the holy man approaches the tomb. Only then does Romeo die, knowing what a terrible error he has made.

Just as in da Porto's and Bandello's versions, it's so much worse if he knows his mistake. If it's going to be about mistiming, let's make it about *mis-timing.*

Now Juliet awakens and finds Romeo dead. The Friar flees, but she refuses to leave her husband. She kisses him, trying to get poison off his lips, to let her die, too. She sits up and utters what is, to me, the most heartbreaking line of the play:

JULIET:
Thy lips are warm.

That's how close they came. Kills me every time.

But there are people coming — the fight with Paris has awakened the watch. She grabs Romeo's dagger from his belt.

JULIET:
Yea, noise? then I'll be brief. O happy dagger!
This is thy sheath; there rust, and let me die.

Most often you see her stab after the word "die", then fall over dead across Romeo's body.

The first time I directed this, my Juliet came to me and asked, "Does a thirteen year-old girl know how to kill herself effectively?"

No, I thought, a sick smile growing. *No, she certainly does not.*

So for that production and several since, Juliet's death has gone like this:

"*O happy dagger! This is thy sheath...*"

She stabs herself in the belly.

It hurts.

She's bleeding.

But she's not dying.

She pushes. It hurts more.

But she can't make it kill her.

There are people coming. She has to die *now*.

But she doesn't have the strength.

She sees Romeo.

She leans over Romeo's body.

She puts the pommel of the dagger on his back.

She uses her own weight to drive herself down onto the dagger's point.

'*There rust and—let—me—die!*'

She dies begging, pleading with the knife to end her life.

Too often directors want to make this pretty. To pose the bodies in a loving embrace. To have them be idyllic, even in death. I think that does a disservice to the audience. If it's pretty, the audience is allowed to think it's the way it's supposed to be. That we condone the fate of these two rash children. They were destined to die, so why not accept it?

I disagree. It has to be awful. It can't be easy. We can't let the audience off the hook that way. This is the ultimate moment of the play. We can't shy away from it.

We have to make it *hurt*.

The Friar's Guilt

A little while back, I reconnected with my high-school Shakespeare teacher from half a lifetime ago. He was also the co-director of my very first production, where, if you remember, I played Mercutio.

He and I wrote back and forth about *The Master of Verona*, but he said he was thinking of me because he was involved in a discussion of why Romeo and Juliet don't just run off together in the middle of the show.

It's a question that always gets to me — in fact, it makes me angry. Not at the play, or at the person asking the question. No, I get mad at a single character in the show: Friar Lawrence.

I hate the Friar. Not as a role. As a person.

There was a musical running here in Chicago a few years back called *The Trial of Friar Lawrence*, humorously blaming him for everything that goes wrong in R&J.

To me, that's not a joke, it's God's honest truth. The blame falls squarely on the Friar's shoulders. Everything he does — and I mean everything! — is done in secret, *sub rosa*, behind men's backs. It is not a flattering portrayal of ecclesiastical meddling.

I grant that the secret wedding is well within the bounds of a normal Shakespeare play, Comedy or Tragedy (*Othello* comes to mind). But the moment Tybalt is killed, the Friar should be on his way to the Prince. "My lord Escalus — these children are married. Do what you can for them." But it doesn't even occur to him! Instead, he comes up with a plan so that Romeo can have his wedding night, then skip town. Romantic, perhaps. But hardly practical — except in a man devoted to secrecy and afraid of being caught.

Why don't Romeo and Juliet flee at that moment? Because of the Friar's counsel. He's the wise authority figure, the man of years. Of course they listen to him.

Then Juliet comes to him, threatening to kill herself unless he can prevent her marriage to Paris. Lawrence swipes a page from Friar Francis in *Much Ado* — fake her death!

Now if it's me (Friar Dave, as it were) here's my plan: "Juliet, I've got a horse out back. Let's get you out of town." But no! Much better to drug her. That way, the secret is still safe.

But the thing I detest the Friar for the most, the single act for which I cannot forgive him, is what happens in the tomb. Discovering Romeo and Paris slain, he hears a noise and fears discovery. He tells the groggy and terrified Juliet to come with him — "I'll dispose of you among a sisterhood of holy nuns!" Even now, he's fearful of the story coming out.

Juliet refuses to leave Romeo. And that's when Lawrence does the unforgivable thing. He leaves her. "I dare no longer stay!" The cowardly friar, the man responsible for her situation, this wise man of years, runs away, leaving a thirteen-year-old girl in her family crypt beside the corpses of her cousin, her fiancé, and her husband. Honestly, what does he think will happen?

It is my sincere hope (and my strict direction when I'm in charge of a production) that when the Prince says some shall be "punished," he's looking directly at Friar Lawrence.

I've played most of the male roles in this show, and there's great fun to be had in them all. Lawrence is no exception. The Friar is a great character to perform. I just loathe him as a person.

Why love Mercutio and revile the Friar? Easy. While Mercutio is wild and troublesome, playing the catalyst in the precipitating event, the disaster that follows is entirely due to the secrecy and fear that pervades the character of Friar Lawrence.

The Death of Benvolio

If you wanted to throw my whole theory about the cause of the feud out of whack, you could point out to me that Lady Montague does not, in fact, have the final death in the play.

I would answer with a nod, a sigh, a smile, saying, "I know. Benvolio does."

In the First Quarto (the 'Bad' Quarto, the 'Eeevil' Quarto) of *Romeo and Juliet*, printed by Thomas Crede for Cuthbert Burby in 1599, Benvolio dies.

What? you cry aloud. How? Why?

Alas, we don't know. Montague brings us news that his wife is dead. Then he adds, as if in after-thought, "And young Benvolio is deceased as well." No word of how or why. All we know is that no one makes it out of this play alive.

I actually like this line. Several times now I've contrived ways to kill Benvolio in the latter part of the play. My favorite is to have him meet a girl at the Capulet party. Later, after Juliet has drunk her potion but before she's found, Benvolio meets this girl for an assignation. They embrace, but she recoils at once. His sword-hilt is jabbing her. Sexily, she either removes his sword belt or unsheathes the weapon and lays it aside.

Just then, unseen by Benvolio, the two louts from the opening scene, Gregory and Sampson, creep up. Benvolio senses them, however, and puts up a desperate fight. But he's unarmed and is quickly killed. It's a nice parallel to the light-hearted melee at the top of the show. Then — ah-ha! — Lady Capulet arrives to pay off her three servants, who then remove the body.

Lady Capulet? Well, she's already told Juliet that she's planning to send a poison to Mantua and have Romeo done in. And she blames Benvolio for spinning a web of lies around the death of Tybalt, despite the fact that he spoke true. Would she let him, "a kinsman to the Montague," live? I think not!

So there's a peek at how my mind works, filling in gaps much like the bootleggers of Shakespeare's time.

I could refute the claim that Benvolio gets the final death by saying that maybe he died days ago, while Lady Montague died this very night. Maybe she sensed her son's passing. Maybe she killed herself for her part in the feud. Maybe she did in fact die of grief. Or maybe she and Benvolio had a sexual-suicide pact and leapt naked off of one of Verona's forty-eight towers.

The world may never know.

Loving Lady Montague

There are lots of choices I've made for Shakespeare's characters in my novels that I've omitted from this volume, as they're extrapolations from the play that don't necessarily help the play in performance. Tybalt being the rightful Capulet heir, usurped by his uncle — it's fun in the novels, and certainly can be played in both Tybalt's hot-headedness and Capulet's lines at the party ("Am I the master here or you!"). Note, too, that Capulet is none too sad to see Tybalt dead. He alone says not a word when Romeo is exiled, while Lady Cap screams her head off.

Still, the majority of the character choices I've made (having the Friar be a Cathar, creating the circumstances for the death of the Nurse's daughter) have no bearing on the play.

Nor does my theory about Lady Montague. And yet she is given so little shape in the play, I include my fleshing-out of her persona here more as a "what-if" than as a guide for performers who want to play.

To reiterate: Lady Montague was supposed to marry Lord Capulet but eloped with Lord Montague instead. The deep friendship between Capulet and Montague was shattered, and the feud began. Boom.

The unintended consequence of crafting this story was that I had to invent a character for Lady Montague, who has a mere two lines in the play. The servant Potpan has a more defined character than Romeo's mother. Hell, unnamed musicians have more personality than she is given. So I had free rein.

I named her Gianozza, the lover who was the prototype for Juliet in Salernitano's *Il Novellino*—as I was setting up a prequel to the famous story of star-cross'd lovers, I liked the idea of using the names from that earlier version of R&J.

And somewhere along the line I ended up creating a character my readers love to hate.

Gianozza's not evil. She's not a schemer or a villain. Instead, in creating her character, I took her son's main failing in the play and decided he learned it from her.

Gianozza's in love with Love.

She's especially fond of love poetry, and becomes fixated with the story of two doomed lovers Dante uses in *Inferno*. She fails to notice that the lovers in question are in Hell. Instead she starts to idealize their doomed romance, with disastrous consequences. She aims to have a great love story just like theirs. And in so doing she sets up a great tragedy.

It all ties into the notion of Courtly Love, of love for love's sake. Dante had his great love, Beatrice. She was not his wife. She was his muse. And when she died, he was able to love her completely, because his love wasn't for the real Beatrice. It was for the idealized version of her.

Courtly Love is great for poetry. It's just lousy for life.

In my novel *The Prince's Doom*, we see Gianozza fifteen years after her marriage to Mariotto Montecchio. By now the marriage is strained. Not because her husband doesn't love her, but because she's no longer the center of attention. The only real attention she gets is from Antony Capulletto, still pining for her after all these years. Unconsciously, she stokes the feud, keeping it alive. There is a moment where Mariotto and Antony could reconcile, renew their friendship, end the feud. But Gianozza can't help inserting herself once again, with disastrous consequences. Instead of burying the feud, she keeps them on the path that will end with them burying their children instead.

But she can't help herself. She has defined herself through being loved by two men, men who are willing to fight and even die for her. She is the new Helen of Troy, the catalyst for great deeds. If she doesn't have that, who is she?

A couple of years ago, Sean Graney adapted all the classic Greek dramas into a single day-long event which he entitled *All Our Tragic*. The title comes from a line that he gives to Clytemnestra: "All our tragic happens because we love someone we shouldn't have."

Truer words were never spoken. Because the best drama doesn't come from hate. It comes from love.

Favorite Play

As I perform and lecture and teach, one question comes up constantly: "What's your favorite Shakespeare play?"

Alongside *Macbeth*, R&J is certainly the play I know best. Definitely the one I have done the most, playing every male role in the show except Paris and Benvolio.

Moreover, it's a show I truly admire. The structure is absolutely flawless. As a piece of theatre, it is entirely perfect.

But it's not something I'm always happy to see, or to do. Kids dying can be like that.

So when I'm asked which Shakespeare play is my favorite, my answer is usually something like this: "As an overall fun play to perform, nothing beats *Much Ado About Nothing*. There are no bad parts, everyone can have a lot of fun, and the audience has a great time. It's also really hard to fuck up."

"But..." they say, hearing the hanging unsaid word.

The "but" is that favorite *play* is different from favorite *role*, which is really what they're asking. Favorite roles? Where do I start? I love playing Benedick, but I also love playing Mac. I've played him so much over the last two decades that he's in my bones now. It's a great part, and a great show.

I used to love Mercutio, back when I was young enough. Petruchio's a blast in a good production — I met my wife playing him. I just got to do Mark Antony in *Caesar*, and I really clicked with him. Hell, I love playing Antonio the Pirate in *Twelfth Night*.

On the other hand, the favorite play question is just as tricky. *Much Ado* is a true answer, but a pat one. Because on the page, and sometimes even on the stage, *Much Ado* pales when compared to *Twelfth Night*.

Twelfth Night is a better Comedy, because it's harder to do right. (Or perhaps it's harder to do right because it's better. Either way.)

First, it has all the Shakespearean Comedic devices: a lovesick man, a smart young woman in distress, clowns, disguises (specifically, a woman-disguised–as-a-man), musicians, secret wedding, mis-timings, mistaken identities, a shipwreck, and twins. This play has all the tropes and standard devices one thinks of in Shakespeare's Comedies. But so often they're done — well, badly.

For example — in the last couple of decades at least, I've seen so many Violas cast because they look like young men. Very KD Lang. To me, that's not the joke. The joke is that, even dressed like a man, Viola is clearly a woman, and Orsino and the rest are idiots for not seeing it. In this, realism is a hindrance. A flat-chested or taped-down Viola is less funny than one whose bosoms Orsino can't see simply because she's dressed like a man. If you have a mannish Viola, then Orsino is gay, and at the end of the play he should be in love with Sebastian, not Viola. You lose an obvious joke.

It's like the twin jokes in *The Comedy of Errors*. If you cast pairs of twins that look too much alike, the audience actually has trouble keeping track of which twin is which. That undermines the comedy of mistaken identity that so much of the play hinges on. It's the characters on stage who should be confused, never the audience.

But that's not the only reason that *Twelfth Night* is a harder — and better — Comedy than *Much Ado*. The jokes are both cleverer and dirtier, more urban and more urbane. There's a lot of heavy language that most Sir Tobys just blow through, not knowing what to do with it. When we did it with the Patches, we were blessed with Ben Montague in the role. Teamed with Andy Carey, Scott Smith, and Jan Blixt as Mariah, Ben made hilarious sense of every word. And the rap that Andy and Ben came up with on their exit one day still plays in my head. (Andy is part of Chicago's Improvised Shakespeare Company. Check them out!)

Lord, now that I'm shouting out performances from that show, it's hard to forget Breon Bliss's original music as Feste, or first Scott Kennedy's then Tom Taylor's Malvolio. Brendan Donaldson's baritone Valentine. And James Elly's show-stealing priest at the end — we had audiences returning with signs made up just for him!

Then there's the whole cast at Michigan Shakespeare Festival's 2013 production, which ended with the most rousing and joyful-crying-singing shared experience I've ever had on stage. Alan Ball was a great Feste in that one, and Paul Riopelle an hilarious Malvolio. Melanie Keller's Viola sparked magnificently off Janet Haley's Olivia, while John Byrnes's Sir Toby in leopard-print leggings and long coat vibed the best and worst of glam rock. Amy Lewis Montgomery's voice tearing out my heart each night singing Katie Hopgood's arrangement of "No Longer Mourn Me When I'm Gone". Brandon Saunders being a touching goofball as Fabian. Dan Helmer stealing the show as Valentine, only to have it stolen from him by Rick Eva eating a banana. I could go on and on…

But back to the show itself. There's also a boatload of clever language about people's roles in society. About love and longing. About putting on airs — everybody in that play is putting on some kind of show, from Orsino's pining to Olivia's mourning, from Viola's disguise to Malvolio's ambitious yellow stockings.

Nobody is what they want others to think they are. And therein lies the fertile land of Comedy.

It's a hard show to do, but if it's done well, it's my favorite Shakespeare play.

Except for...

A Prayer Before Dying

Sometimes I'm not asked my favorite play or my favorite role. Sometimes I'm asked my favorite *moment* in Shakespeare.

Dear lord.

Having performed about two-thirds of the canon, there are plenty to choose from. As mentioned earlier, I tend to lean toward the heartbreaking. Juliet's line to dead Romeo: "Thy lips are warm." Or maybe Kent holding dead Lear: "Vex not his ghost. O, let him pass." Things like that.

But my favorite moment in all of Shakespeare, the one that kills me every time, is from *Othello*. Perversely, it's a line that is almost always cut in performance.

By Act V, our Tragic hero is utterly convinced that his faithful wife is anything but — that she has been carrying on with Cassio. But he still loves her; if he did not, he could not be so passionately moved. So, though he has resolved to kill her, he first must make certain she has prayed:

OTHELLO:
Have you pray'd tonight, Desdemona?

DESDEMONA:
Ay, my lord.

OTHELLO:
If you bethink yourself of any crime
Unreconciled as yet to heaven and grace,
Solicit for it straight.

DESDEMONA:
Alas, my lord, what do you mean by that?

OTHELLO:
Well, do it, and be brief; I will walk by:
I would not kill thy unprepared spirit;
No; heaven forfend! I would not kill thy soul.

DESDEMONA:
Talk you of killing?

OTHELLO:
Ay, I do.

DESDEMONA:
Then heaven
Have mercy on me!

OTHELLO:
Amen, with all my heart!

Why does Othello care if she prayed? Elizabethan tradition held that a prayer before dying will cleanse the soul, sending it to Heaven. It's actually a rather Lutheran belief, not needing a priest to intercede between penitent and God. This same belief stops Hamlet from murdering his uncle while Claudius is bent in prayer. Here, Othello is making sure that, though she must die, Desdemona's soul will go to paradise. His passion and his honor demand her death, but his love demands her soul be saved.

He kills her, smothering her with a pillow — twice. Although when I last staged it, the second time he goes to kill her, I had him tenderly hold her, then break her neck. This is because, like so many Shakespearean characters, she must talk after she is murdered. Mercutio does this, and Paris, and young Macduff, and countless others — they are dead, and speaking their last. So, too, does Desdemona. But a woman smothered to death is unlikely to speak, hence my choice to have her die slowly of a broken neck.

Her maid Emilia rushes into the room and kneels beside her dying mistress, while Othello looks on:

EMILIA:
Out, and alas! that was my lady's voice.
Help! help, ho! help! O lady, speak again!
Sweet Desdemona! O sweet mistress, speak!

DESDEMONA:
A guiltless death I die.

EMILIA:
O, who hath done this deed?

DESDEMONA:
Nobody; I myself. Farewell.
Commend me to my kind lord: O, farewell!

That! That right there is my favorite line in Shakespeare! "Nobody; I myself."

Desdemona loves Othello so much, so deeply and truly, that even as she's dying she tells this lie for him. Her love is deeper than Othello's because it can forgive anything — even her own murder.

Here's why this moment wreaks havoc on me. By saying she did it, she is telling a lie. Thus committing a sin. Thus damning her soul to Hell to protect the man who just murdered her. Desdemona willingly condemns herself to eternal damnation to save Othello. It's so awfully, wonderfully Tragic I can hardly breathe.

As I mentioned, this moment is hardly ever staged. It's too hard, or too funny, to have a murdered woman talk. But staged properly, it has all the more power, because it shows the depth of the love Othello has just cast away.

It's my favorite moment in all of Shakespeare.

Coffee with the Count

By Janice L Blixt

In *The Master of Verona*, the title "Count" is reserved for the villain, the historical Count of San Bonifacio. But when David mentions the Count to me, I respond with a smile and a joke about pouring coffee.

David and I got married in 2002. Our honeymoon also served as a research trip for him. Of the three months we spent touring Europe, starting in Greece and ending in London, fully a month was spent in Italy. Of that month, a week was spent in Verona. Thanks to the advice of a friend, photojournalist David Turnley, he'd been in contact with Antonella Leonardo, Assistant Minister of Culture. She arranged every meeting we had in Verona. It was June, and Italy was experiencing a major heat wave, so there were a lot of dinners.

The first time we met her, she gave us a list of places to go and people to talk to, and, in passing, handed David a card, saying, "And, of course, you'd like to talk to the Count of Serego-Alighieri. He still lives on the estate purchased by Dante's son."

Well, yes… of course we would… ummm… wow… the Count has a card. Ok.

So we sat on the bed in our hotel room debating just what one should say to a Count when one calls to set up a chat. Finally deciding our natural paralysis was a bit ridiculous, David, in a burst of confidence and devil-may-care energy, called the number we had been given… and reached the Count's teenaged daughter. "Pronto."

David said something like, "I'm looking for the, uh, Count?"

"My father isn't here. Leave your name and he'll ring you back."

Minutes later the phone trilled, and I leapt for it. "Hello?"

"Hello. This is the Count Serego-Alighieri."

"Hi! Um, my name is David Blixt. I'm writing a book about Shakespeare and Dante, and one of the main characters is Dante's son, Pietro. I was, ah, wondering if I could come out and — speak to you."

"How long are you in Verona?"

"Until Saturday."

"Come up tomorrow morning. 10 o'clock. Yes?"

"Yes! We'll be there!"

"Ring the bell."

That night, David and I had a wonderful dinner with a couple of college professors, true academics and Marxists to the core. The meal was lovely — other than the argument we had when we mentioned our next day's excursion: "Italy is a democracy! There are no Counts anymore!"

Well, okay then… But we were still set to meet the direct descendant of Dante Alighieri at the home and vineyard Pietro Alighieri purchased in 1353! Call us star-struck, but that was pretty cool in our minds. We whispered to each other in the cab on the way home from dinner, "And he is SO a Count."

The next morning we took a cab from our hotel to the address we had been given, many miles outside of the city, down winding country roads. The cabbie stopped the car next to a rather nondescript 15 foot high stone wall. In garbled Itanglish, we asked "Is this it?" He nodded and pointed at the wall.

As the cab drove away, David noticed that there were some buzzer buttons placed high on the wall — the kind you find at the front door of many Chicago three-flats, little white buttons with little white name-tags made on a labeling machine next to them. They said things like "Vineyard Business Office" and "First Floor Office" — in Italian, of course. One said "Count Serego-Alighieri." Giggling like five-year-olds, we pressed that button. After a moment, a low voice came over a small speaker, "Si?"

Immediately sobering, David said, "Hello. My name is David Blixt, and I have an appointment to meet with the Count." After a pause, "Si, yes, turn the corner and go in the vineyard office."

About twenty feet from the little buttons, the wall made a turn. We walked to that point and saw that where the wall seemed to end was a door into a large, rustic, wood-paneled and beamed room full of racks and barrels — the walls covered with bottles of wine and vinegar. There was a counter on one wall with two young women wrapping bottles for shipment and a desk near a door on the far side of the room with a young man who appeared to be doing accounts. The workers in the room barely glanced up. David and I stood in the dim room nervously waiting — for what, we weren't sure.

A moment or two later, the far door opened and a man entered. He was of medium height, slight of weight, and had straight brown hair, greying at the temples, in an expensive cut. He was wearing a linen button-down white shirt with the sleeves rolled to the elbows and open at the neck and grey linen trousers. He looked at the two of us and approached with a hand outstretched. "Hello, I am Piere-Alvins Serego-Alighieri, and you must be David and Mrs. Blixt." We nodded and smiled as David shook hands with him, and he nodded in greeting to me. "Why don't we go into the house?" And he turned and walked towards the door from which he came.

The Count lead us into a large paved-in-stones courtyard framed by the vineyard building we had just left, a large, square barn-like building, a long, two-storied stone building, and the house.

The house! A lovely Italian stone house that looked both fresh and inviting and also as if it had been there forever, carved out of the countryside. It had large double doors in the center of the first floor that led us into a two-story entryway. The marble floor was polished to an almost mirror-like sheen, the center of the floor containing an inlaid heraldic crest. David and I skirted the crest, trying to study it and the rest of the room surreptitiously while following the Count. He noticed our appraisal of the floor and said, "That was updated in the 1470s when the Serego family married the Alighieri. It was originally just the Alighieri symbol — now it is much more."

David told him that the main character of his book was Pietro Alighieri and that we were very interested in the home that he had built — and were fascinated to discover his descendant still lived there.

The Count smiled briefly. "Then you will appreciate this." He opened a large cabinet against a wall in the entryway and pulled out a poster-sized piece of parchment. He held it up for us to see, and as we tried to decipher the Italian of the document, he said, "The original deed to the property." Seriously. He just happened to have a document from the fourteenth century in a cabinet in his entryway. "Let me show you around."

Piere-Alvins Serego-Alighieri is an elegant man. I can't think of any other word to describe him. He is soft-spoken, his low voice easy to hear and relaxed with a lovely Italian accent to his fluent English. He uses his hands occasionally as he speaks — not in the stereotypical Mediterranean style, but simply, casually, with fluid motions from the wrists. He's the kind of man who seems to use no excess energy as he moves or speaks — he is perfectly balanced and perfectly calm and perfectly natural in the incredible grace of his home. He smoked quite a bit while we were there, but the smoking had a quiet, cavalier quality instead of the rat-like energy most Americans have when they smoke.

We followed him through his home, through rooms that had been decorated in the fourteenth century and redecorated throughout the centuries since. Antiques from seven centuries lived together in this house. As we walked from room to room, I was reminded of the different villas and homes and museums we had toured in our travels that summer and felt these rooms were no less opulent or stylish, their contents no less rare or extraordinary than the rooms that were blocked off by red velvet ropes to preserve their treasures. And, interesting to me, mixed in among the fifteenth and nineteenth-century antique chairs, tables, paintings, and chests were CDs and a new stereo system on a console table, family photos in bright plastic frames, and recently published paperbacks and magazines on a sofa here or on a desk there. In the midst of this museum of a house was a home, with a teenaged girl living there. Amazing.

We ended up in a small study (small being a relative word choice. It was smaller than some of the rooms we'd been in, but larger than our Chicago apartment). This one held the wedding coaches the bride and the groom rode in when the Alighieris married the Seregos. Like the entry foyer, this room had a crest in the stone floor and also a large fireplace and floor-to-ceiling French doors. We sat on an upholstered settee, and the Count sat across a large coffee table from us in a leather club chair.

He and David discussed some of the history of the Alighieri family while I tried not to gape at the room. Apparently, the Alighieri sons had the tendency, in the generations following Pietro, to join the priesthood, and by the late fifteenth century, there were no marriageable males left. At that point in the family's history, there was only one daughter, the sons both having taken holy orders. The daughter was courted by a Count Serego, and, when he asked her brothers for permission to marry her, they agreed on one condition — that they not allow the name of Dante Alighieri to die out. They would give the Count their sister if, in return, he took their name and passed it along to their children. It was at this time that the family became Serego-Alighieri.

At this point in the conversation, the Count switched gears and asked, "Would you like coffee?" He then stood, walked over to the door, and called "Marco!" out into the hall. A pause. "Marco!" He then spoke quietly to someone in the hallway and then returned to his seat.

David asked a question about the original size of the land purchase, and they continued their discussion. After a few minutes, a tall man in a suit appeared in the doorway with a tray and silver coffee service. The Count stopped his narrative while the man placed the tray on the coffee table. "Grazie, Marco," he murmured as the man left the room. The Count then picked up his description of the original planting of the vineyards where he had left off.

David and the Count chatted on for a while as I continued to look around the room and admire the small pieces around me. After a couple of minutes, I wondered about the coffee. It was just sitting there on the table between us. The Count's manservant (his manservant!... teehee) didn't appear to be coming back.

And then it occurred to me — I am woman.

Hear me roar.

Oh — and the Count seemed to be waiting for me to pour. Seriously.

I was sitting in a fourteenth-century villa in the Italian countryside with my husband and a Count, and they were expecting me to pour their coffee.

After a few calming breaths and a mental gathering of the all the societal mores I'd culled from Jane Austen's novels, I reached out and took the handle of the coffee pot and asked, "Shall I pour?"

The Count waved assent with one cigaretted hand and continued to talk to David about the outbuildings and when they were added to the original plan.

I sat on the settee with the coffee pot in one hand, picking up the cups and saucers in the other and trying to keep my hands still enough that the china didn't rattle as I asked at appropriate breaks in the conversation, "How do you like your coffee?"

The Count likes his with a little cream.

Somehow I managed to serve, feeling like I was having tea with the Queen. And feeling incredibly American and incredibly twenty-first century. And feeling a little bit angry with my feminist self who wouldn't shut up and stop whispering in my ear, *Why can't he pour his own damn coffee?*

I've told this story for years. But there is a wonderful coda.

We visited again in 2014, twelve years after our honeymoon trip. The city of Verona had flown David out for a book release, and while we were there, the Count had graciously offered to have us stay at his home for a couple of nights.

We had drinks and discussed the history of the vineyard some more. The Count regaled us with a terrific story about how the villa survived WWII — you should get David to tell it to you. Then the Count asked us if we had plans for dinner. We hadn't. Sadly, he was engaged that evening, but he would see if he could make a restaurant reservation for us.

At 7 a taxi arrived for us, with the Count picking up the fare. We were driven up a very high hill to a marvelous restaurant with a view of Lake Garda and the whole Valpolicella region. Asked where we'd like to sit, we chose the patio outside.

Looking around, we noted that the restaurant was curiously empty. We'd lost track of the time, like you do when you're traveling. It was a Monday, the day most restaurants in Italy are closed.

Apparently the Count had his man Paulo make a phone call and ask the restaurant to open. Just for us.

It was a glorious meal, and we felt better once other people started arriving—seeing the restaurant was open, they had decided to come in. But the Count picked up our bill, treating us to a marvelous four-course meal, the only time in my life when I've taken photos of my food.

There is a certain entitlement to old money, to be sure. It can be infuriating. It can also be generous.

I love the quote from *The Philadelphia Story*: "With the rich and powerful, always a little patience."

Resources

In the past twenty years I've amassed quite a collection of books about R&J, Verona, and related subjects. But there are four to which I turn most often.

The first is my facsimile copy of Shakespeare's First Folio, a volume I go to every time I start work on a play. Seeing the choices in punctuation, in spelling, in capitalization — it's like being directed by Shakespeare. The fact that more people don't know how to read the Folio is deeply depressing to me. It's like we're cypher clerks, a sea of Robert Langdons, decoding the most important text to which only a few have the key.

Second up, and just as valuable, is *Asimov's Guide to Shakespeare* by Isaac Asimov. The man never slept, I'm sure of it. It's the only way to explain his incredible output of well-researched material on such a wide variety of subjects. This is the book we buy non-Shakespeare people who are interested in knowing more about his plays. And yet even the most knowledgeable Shakespearean can find new and wonderful twists on history and performance in here. It's a must-have.

Next is a thin volume I was lucky enough to stumble upon. It's a collection of differing versions of *Romeo & Juliet* (ironically published by the Dante University Press). It includes the works by Masuccio, Luigi da Porto, Bandello, and, of course, Shakespeare. It is basic, but no less invaluable for that.

Lastly there's the first volume of *Narrative and Dramatic Sources for Shakespeare*, which reprints Arthur Brooke's (long, awful, boring!) *Tragicall Historye of Romeus and Juliet*. It also provides another history of the sequence of the release of plays, which I've relied on heavily for my chapter entitled "Sources."

I also frequently crack open *Shakespeare's Songbook* by Ross W. Duffin, from whose references to music in the play I've learned so much.

From here we move into more general Verona information, the most important of which was A. M. Allen's century-old *A History of Verona*. Though Ms. Allen takes much legend as pure fact, her analyses of events and insights into the people and their politics are fascinating. She also has several lovely turns of phrase, making her book an enjoyable, as well as informative, read. I also quite enjoyed *Padua Under the Carrara* by Benjamin G. Kohl. And for an overview of the era, Barbara Tuchman's *A Distant Mirror* is utterly terrific.

For details of Dante's family history, I relied greatly upon *Dante e Gli Allighieri a Verona* by Emanuele Carli. For more personal information, I was honored with an interview with Count Serego-Alighieri, which my wife recounts in "Coffee with the Count."

For Dante's own work, I've read the Longfellow, the Oxford, and the Penguin translations of *Inferno*. But best is the one by Robert and Jean Hollander, and their commentary is magnificent (though not for the faint of heart).

The Dante Encyclopedia is also terrific, not only as a codex to *The Divine Comedy*, but also as a rough 'who's who' for the era in which R&J takes place.

Harriet Rubin's *Dante in Love* came in during the final edits to give me a little period flavor — which side of the hat Guelphs wore their feathers on, etc. And Alison Cornish's *Reading Dante's* offers a look into the astrology of the period.

Many of my other source texts were in Italian, German, or Latin. When this is the case, it behooves one to read these languages with something that resembles fluency. Though my Italian has improved greatly, I was still often forced to rely on translators. For their work in this capacity, I must thank Sylvia Giorgini (Italian), Professor Martin Walsh (German), and my old high school chum, Professor John Lober, for his help with a bit of Latin.

Then there are the living Veronese. Antonella Leonardo at the Ministry of Culture was unbelievably kind and helpful, answering questions and arranging for my wife and me to meet a half dozen fascinating people while we stayed. It was due to Antonella that we were invited to visit Count Serego-Alighieri.

Antonella also connected me with Professor Rita Severi. Rita teaches at the University of Verona. She, her husband Paolo, and their lovely daughter Giulia took us out for the single most enjoyable evening in a three-month tour of Europe. I learned more about Verona in that night than in two years of reading. Rita led me to the city library, where I was inundated with books as a gift from the head librarian. I am very much in her debt.

Two days later, we were taken on another tour by Daniela Zumiani, who showed us the Roman ruins under the city, available through shop basements and restaurant wine cellars. In her honor, let me plug her book, *Shakespeare and Verona—Palaces and Courtyards of Medieval Verona*, available in both English and Italian.

Any errors are, of course, mine.

Of course, none of this would be possible without the words, wit, and wisdom of William Shakespeare.

Author Biography

Consistently described as "intricate," "taut," and "breathtaking," David Blixt's written work combines a love of theatre with a deep respect for the quirks and passions of history. His novels span the early Roman Empire (the *Colossus* series, his play *Eve of Ides*) to early Renaissance Italy (the *Star-Cross'd* series) up through the Elizabethan era with *Her Majesty's Will*. His latest novel, *What Girls Are Good For: A Novel of Nellie Bly* explores the early career of the famous pioneer of undercover reporting.

As an actor, David has made a career out of Shakespeare, with special attention to *Romeo & Juliet*, in which he has played every major male role save Benvolio. Other favorite roles include Macbeth, Iachimo in *Cymbeline*, Benedick in *Much Ado About Nothing*, Mark Antony in *Julius Caesar*, Petruchio in *The Taming of the Shrew*, Leontes in *The Winter's Tale*, Kent in *King Lear*, and Orsino in *Twelfth Night*. David is the resident fight director for two Shakespeare companies and for eight years has taught stage combat at the Chicago High School For The Arts.

An Artistic Associate of the Michigan Shakespeare Festival, David continues to write, act, and travel. He has ridden camels around the pyramids at Giza, been thrown out of the Vatican Museum and been blessed by Pope John-Paul II, scaled the Roman ramp at Masada, crashed a hot-air balloon, leapt from cliffs on small Greek islands, dined with Counts and criminals, climbed to the top of Mount Sinai, and sat in the Prince's chair in Verona's palace. But David is happiest at his desk, weaving tales of brilliant people in dire and dramatic straits.

Living in Chicago with his wife and two children, David describes himself as "actor, author, father, husband. In reverse order."

www.davidblixt.com

Other Books by David Blixt

Shakespeare's Secrets: Macbeth

THE STAR-CROSS'D SERIES
 The Master Of Verona
 Voice Of The Falconer
 Fortune's Fool
 The Prince's Doom
 Varnished Faces - Star-Cross'd Short Stories

THE COLOSSUS SERIES
 Colossus: Stone & Steel
 Colossus: The Four Emperors
 COMING SOON
 Colossus: Wail of the Fallen

Her Majesty's Will
What Girls Are Good For: A Novel of Nellie Bly
Eve Of Ides – a play of Brutus and Caesar
Fighting Words– a Combat Glossary, by Blixt, Girard, Kirby, & Leoni

Lightning Source UK Ltd.
Milton Keynes UK
UKHW022031150121
377139UK00011B/512/J